PUFFIN BOOKS

TRAPPED IN ICE

Eric Walters is the author of four children's books including *Stand Your Ground,* a regional winner of the Silver Birch Award, and *S.T.A.R.S.,* which also won a Silver Birch Award. He is an elementary school teacher and lives in Mississauga with his wife and three children.

TRAPPED IN ICE

by

ERIC WALTERS

Puffin Books

PUFFIN BOOKS
Published by the Penguin Group
Penguin Books Canada Ltd, 10 Alcorn Avenue, Toronto, Ontario,
Canada M4V 3B2
Penguin Books Ltd, 27 Wrights Lane, London W8 5TZ, England
Penguin Putnam Inc., 375 Hudson Street, New York, New York 10014,
U.S.A.
Penguin Books Australia Ltd, Ringwood, Victoria, Australia
Penguin Books (NZ) Ltd, cnr Rosedale and Airborne Roads, Albany,
Auckland 1310, New Zealand

Penguin Books Ltd, Registered Offices:
Harmondsworth, Middlesex, England

First published in Viking by Penguin Books Canada Limited, 1997
Published in Puffin Books, 1999
5 7 9 10 8 6 4

*Publisher's note: This book is a work of fiction. Names, characters,
places and incidents either are the product of the author's imagination
or are used fictitiously, and any resemblance to actual persons living
or dead, events, or locales is entirely coincidental.*

Manufactured in Canada

Canadian Cataloguing in Publication Data

Walters, Eric, 1957–
Trapped in ice

ISBN 0-14-038626-2

1. Arctic regions – Discovery and exploration – Canadian
– Juvenile fiction. I. Title

PS8595.A598T72 1998   jC813'.54   C96–932396-4
PZ7.W34Tr 1998

Visit Penguin Canada's web site at **www.penguin.ca**

*This novel is dedicated to the spirit of
Captain Robert Bartlett*

*a*CKNOWLEDGMENTS

This novel was completed while my family and I stayed with friends in Nova Scotia. I'd like to thank the Davidson family for opening their home and their hearts and for allowing parts of their past and personalities to become embedded in my characters.

pREFACE

❄

This novel is based on the real-life adventure of Captain Robert Bartlett and the Canadian Arctic Expedition of 1913. The plot follows actual events and is true to the essence of the story. However, most of the characters, with the exception of Robert Bartlett, were known to me only by name and it was necessary to imagine their personalities. This is especially true for my main character, Helen, who tells the story. Much more information was available concerning Captain Bartlett, and I hope my portrayal accurately reflects his courage, integrity, intelligence, determination and strength.

300 MI.
300 KM.

Arctic Ocean

Shipwreck Camp

Wrangel Is.

Herald I.

Sled Journeys

Arctic Circle

Siberia

the "Karluk"

Point Hop

Bering Strait

Senki

Nome

the "Karluk"

St. Lawrence I.

St. Mich

St. Matthew Is.

Bering Sea

Nunivak Is.

Voyage of the "Karluk" from Vancouver

N
W   E
S

path of the "Karluk" adrift in the ice

Banks Is.

Victoria Is.

Herschel Is.

District of Mackenzie

Point Barrow

Arctic Circle

Mackenzie

Yukon

Alaska

British Columbia

Juneau

Gulf of Alaska

from Vancouver

Karluk Expedition 1913-1914

TRAPPED IN ICE

❄

1

July 1913

The carriage travelled slowly through the streets, the clip-clop of the horses' hooves against the cobblestones the only thing marking our movement. Our ride was smooth, smoother than any wagon I'd ever been in before. It was cushioned by special rubber wheels, like the kind used by the new horseless carriages. I would have loved to have had a spin in one of those, but I was just grateful to be in a coach as fancy as this.

We had boarded this carriage at the train station, where two porters had helped us move all our boxes and bags. This hadn't surprised me because we had so much to carry. We had all our clothes and personal belongings and some toys, and of course the books we'd need to do our schooling. Mother had told us we might be going away for two years but we weren't getting away from school. It would just mean she'd be our teacher.

What shocked me, though, was when Mother had told the porters to stop beside this coach. I thought we shouldn't be so extravagant, but she said it was important to travel to our ship first class. After all, she'd said, it wasn't every day you become part of the Canadian Arctic Expedition.

I'd seen carriages like this before but never dreamed that I'd be riding in one. It had polished wood and silver fittings. Inside were special soft upholstered seats and little curtains hanging in the windows and kerosene lamps. I wished it was night so the driver would light the lamps. The two horses pulling us had gleaming coats and elaborate reins and bridles and the driver was dressed fancier than anybody I'd ever seen except in pictures. He looked like a prince going to a fancy ball with the Queen of England. And I felt a bit like Cinderella.

Of course, Cinderella only had two wicked stepsisters. She didn't know how lucky she was not to have a little brother. Sitting in this fine carriage, reading my book, I was trying to act dignified and ladylike but my brother was practically hanging out the window gawking at the sights. It wasn't just that he was embarrassing me, as always, but he kept on blocking my view as he bounced from side to side. It wasn't fair! He wasn't the only one who had never been in Vancouver before.

There were hundreds and hundreds of people and automobiles sputtering and spewing out smoke. I even saw buildings more than five stories high. On one side, over the top of my brother's head, I could make out the tall masts of sailing ships, all docked or anchored along the shore or at the piers lining the waterfront.

"Mother, can't you make him sit down?" I pleaded.

"He's just excited, Helen."

"He could still act more grown up."

"Your brother is only eleven, Helen."

"I just think he could—"

"Stop right now, Helen! Put down that book and enjoy the sights."

I closed my book and placed it on my lap.

I always have a book with me. Mother insists I read what she calls "classic literature" or books filled with science facts. She disapproves of the stories I like which are filled with adventure and excitement, but she doesn't stop me from reading them. She calls them "pulp" and "trash." Since Father's death we haven't been able to afford any new books so I've just reread my favourites over and over. It would truly be nice to have some new books, but reading one I know is almost like visiting a friend.

I felt the carriage sway to one side and the sound of the horses' hooves changed tones. They were no longer hitting cobblestones but echoing against wooden beams. I leaned forward in my seat and pushed the window curtain aside so I could see better. We were on a wide wooden pier. Michael moved over, and tried to look through my window. Reluctantly I let him squeeze his head under my arm.

We were rolling along a pier, past ships moored right up to the dock. Some of them had tall masts, their sails all furled up, while others had high metal walls and were driven by engines. There were lots of men scrambling around, some using cargo nets to load or unload the ships. There was no telling what cargos they carried or where the ships had travelled from. I'd read so many stories about adventures around the world. Maybe these ships had come from China or Australia or San Francisco or—

"Whoaaa!" came the driver's voice through the window and the carriage stopped.

"We're here!" Michael exclaimed as he opened the door and jumped out. I quickly followed him, anxious to catch my first look at the ship we'd be sailing on. Michael ran over to the edge of the pier.

"Is this it?" He pointed to a ship tied to the dock directly in front of us.

"I don't know." I turned to face Mother, who was climbing down out of the carriage. "Is this it?"

"I don't think so, Helen. It looks too old, and not large enough for an expedition of this magnitude," she answered.

The ship seemed pretty big to me, although I did agree it looked awfully old. It was a wooden sailing ship—long and thin with two huge masts towering over our heads. The rigging and ropes reached down from the masts to the deck, which sat below the level of the pier. I could just see a hint of sails furled and tucked away underneath canvas.

The carriage driver started to take down our luggage.

"Wait a minute!" said Mother. "Are you sure this is the *Karluk*?"

"This is where you told me to bring you," he answered, continuing to unload our baggage. "Pier fifty-two, berth five."

"But this surely can't be the *Karluk*."

"Don't know whether it is or isn't. I know this is where you asked me to take you," he replied, as he removed two more bags and placed them on the pier.

"But…" she stammered.

"Why don't we ask that man?" Michael interrupted, pointing to a sailor who had just come up onto the deck of the ship.

Mother walked over and called out, "EXCUSE ME!"

The sailor who stood below us wore a large baggy sweater and ragged pants. He couldn't have been more than sixteen years old.

"Yes, ma'am?"

"Could you tell me where we could find the *Karluk*?"

"Ya found 'er, ma'am, right 'ere under your eyes."

I turned to Mother, and was struck by her look of confusion. I think the sailor saw the same expression.

"Somethin' wrong, ma'am?"

"Ah…no…I just…do you think you could help us move some things aboard?" she asked.

"Sure t'ing," he answered. He climbed up a ladder and joined us on the dock. His hands and face were covered in dirt and grease and his dark hair was soaked with sweat. Even amongst all the other smells along the dock I could make out the stench of his sweat. He'd obviously been working hard. He stared at the small mountain of boxes and bags on the pier beside the carriage.

"I'm Jonathan Brady, ma'am. Me friends call me Jonnie. And who would ya all be?"

"My name is Mrs. Kiruk and these are my two children, Helen and Michael."

He wiped his filthy hands on his equally filthy sweater and then reached out and shook our hands.

"An' who is all of this stuff for?" Jonnie asked, spreading his arms out over our things.

"It's all ours," Michael answered.

"Yours?"

"Yes, ours. Things we'll be needing on this expedition," Mother replied.

"Ya don't mean ya'll be comin' along with us?"

"Of course. I'm the seamstress and my children will be accompanying me on this trip."

Jonnie looked even more puzzled. "Does the Cap'n know about all of this?"

"I don't know about the Captain. I was hired by the leader of the expedition, Mr. Vilhjalmur Stefansson," Mother answered.

Mother had said Mr. Stefansson's name with a sense of pride. She'd told us all about him: how he was a world-famous Arctic explorer and hero. She'd said I could meet a real-life hero instead of those phoney characters I was always reading about.

"Yes, ma'am...but does the Cap'n know?"

"That would be a matter between Mr. Stefansson and the Captain. Are you going to help move our things?" asked Mother.

"Course, ma'am," he replied, picking up the first of our possessions and starting down the ladder with a heavy trunk on his shoulder. Michael and I both picked up a couple of small bags and followed him. I hesitated at the top. I didn't think I could hold the bag and balance myself going down the ladder, especially while wearing my best dress, which was long and bulky.

"Move over," Michael called out, pushing me slightly off to the side.

I watched enviously as he glided down the ladder. He was like a little monkey and had no fear of falling. He was always climbing over fences, onto the roofs of buildings and up to the top of trees. I thought he was happiest when he was in the highest branches, swaying in the breeze. Where we were going, up to the high Arctic, there aren't any trees. When Mother had told Michael, he'd said he wasn't going to go.

For me, I could care less about any old trees. I was sad to leave my friends behind and I was looking forward to going into eighth form. Even worse, it wasn't like I could be sure of making new friends. Where we were going there might not even be anybody my age...

probably no other children ... except for my brother. I guess in some ways it really didn't matter. We had to go somewhere, whether it was here or someplace else.

Michael jumped down the bottom three or four rungs of the ladder and landed noisily on the deck. I watched from up above, clutching the bag, trying to figure out what I was going to do.

"Here, toss it down," Jonnie called.

I held onto the top railing of the ladder, leaned over and dropped the bag. He caught it gently in his arms.

"I'll get a cargo net an' we can bring 'em all down with the boom," Jonnie suggested.

Mother walked over to my side and placed an arm around my waist.

"Don't be disappointed, dear. This is only the transportation to our new home. I'm sure it will be all right."

"I'm not disappointed ... not too disappointed anyway."

Mother smiled. "I know it's not like those fine ships in all those books."

That was certainly true. The ships in the books I read were always graceful and dignified and fit for royalty. This was just a tramp ship.

"And even though it's an old ship I'm sure it's safe," she continued.

I nodded, although until she tried to reassure me I hadn't thought there was even a possibility it wouldn't be safe. Now I was worried.

Mother and I carried a couple of the bags, those that weren't too heavy, over to the edge of the pier. Meanwhile Jonnie swung the boom over and lowered a net onto the dock. As he loaded our bags into the net, Mother supervised from above, giving him directions and explaining what was fragile and what needed to stay upright.

I wandered along the pier to the back end of the ship to check the name. I'd read about pirates, and I worried that we might be "shanghaied" and sold into white slavery or killed on the high seas or... But there was the name in faded red paint—*Karluk*.

I was now far enough away that I couldn't hear what Mother was saying any more, but I could see Jonnie shaking his head in agreement. I walked back towards them and I could hear him saying, "Yes, ma'am" or "No, ma'am," and I figured he was pretty smart to listen to what she had to say. Mother is a very determined woman...at least she is now.

Before Father died, I'd always seen her as being gentle and soft and kind to a fault. But now she was different. It was as if she just didn't have the time to laugh or smile. She always seemed to be doing one thing or another, or to be worried about something. I never thought she approved of Father giving Michael the belt when he needed it, and believe me he did need it, but she's taken the switch to him a few times this past year herself.

Once everything was secured in the cargo net to Mother's satisfaction, Jonnie went back onto the ship to work the boom. Michael and I followed closely behind him. From the deck I looked up and saw Mother climbing down the ladder. The folds of her green dress billowed around her, revealing wisps of petticoat underneath. It was obvious her dress, her best dress, was not suited for such activities. Her hat was perched precariously atop her head, held in place with a hatpin. Jonnie noticed her coming down and scrambled over to offer assistance. I knew there was no way she was going to accept his help. I didn't hear what she said, but he turned away with a look on his face like a dog that had just been hit with a rolled-up newspaper. I knew that look from the inside.

Jonnie skilfully lifted the cargo up into the air, swung it over the side of the ship, and gently lowered it to the deck. It was all done so smoothly that even Mother couldn't find anything to object to.

"Jonathan…Jonathan Cornelius Brady!" called out a voice.

I spun around.

"Where are ya? Lazin' about with work ta be done!" The voice was coming from below deck.

As soon as Jonnie leaped down from the boom, a man emerged from the hatchway.

"Jonathan, ya best get back ta your work or…" The man stopped in mid-sentence as he spied the three of us standing there. A black woollen cap hid the top part of his face, while a scruffy dark beard covered the bottom half. He walked towards us.

As he got closer, I could tell he was a lot older than Jonnie, maybe even as old as my mother. He had on blue dungarees, a filthy white sweater and a bandanna around his neck. Jonnie ran up to him and started to explain things, but was brushed off with a gesture. The man stopped directly in front of us, a puzzled look on his face, and studied us as if we were some sort of display at the World Exposition. I looked away when his piercing brown eyes caught mine.

"An' who may ya all be?" he asked.

"I'm Mrs. Kiruk."

I expected him to reach out his hand and introduce himself the way Jonnie had done. Instead his face became even more troubled.

"An' what's your business here?"

"I am in the employment of the Canadian Arctic Expedition. I am the seamstress."

"You're the seamstress? An' these two?" he asked, pointing at me and Michael.

"These are my two children," Mother answered, her eyes focused directly on this man.

He looked down at us. "How old are ya?" he asked me.

"I'm thirteen, sir," I answered.

"An' your brother?"

"Almost eleven," Michael chimed in.

"Thirteen an' almost eleven," he said shaking his head sadly. "It's not right for a mother ta be leavin' her children alone for two years…isn't right."

"She's not leaving us," said Michael. "We're going along."

"What!" the man snapped. "Are my ears not workin' right, Jonathan? Has all that bangin' of boards we've been doin' caused my ears ta stop workin'?" he asked, turning to Jonnie. "These little ones think they're goin' along?"

"They are coming along, I can assure you, sir!" said Mother firmly.

I could tell by her tone, the way she said "sir," that she was not favourably impressed with this man.

"I only accepted this position if my children could be part of the trip and Mr. Stefansson readily agreed. It is all confirmed in this telegram."

Mother opened her purse and produced the telegram. She handed it to the man. He squinted his eyes and his bushy black eyebrows almost met as he studied it intently. He looked up.

"She's not tellin' lies, Jonathan. It does say right

here she was offered the job an' her children are comin' along. Now I just have one more question. I need ta know who the bigger fool is, Stefansson for offering ta take her children, or her for askin' for them to come in the first place." He handed the telegram back to my mother. Her mouth and eyes opened wide in shock. He turned away. Over his shoulder he called out to Jonnie, "Too much ta be done ta waste time lollygaggin' around."

Mother continued to stand there, in shock. I had never seen her at a loss for words. I couldn't imagine her allowing such a crude and unfair comment against either her or Mr. Stefansson.

"EXCUSE ME!" yelled Mother to the retreating sailor, who spun around at her words.

"Is it your custom to speak ill of people who are not present? People like Mr. Stefansson?" she asked.

"If he was here he'd be hearin' my words himself."

"Brave words. Would you still be so brave if I was to tell him of your comments?" asked Mother.

The man chuckled. "Ya go right up ta the end of the pier, turn left an' go ta the Four Anchors Hotel. You'll find Mr. Stefansson there, makin' plans for the voyage. You go an' tell him my words an' save me a trip. I've got too much ta be done ta go an' tell him myself."

"And who should I say was questioning his directions?" Mother continued.

"Ya just tell him it was Bob…Bob Bartlett."

"I'm sure Mr. Stefansson will be very displeased. Perhaps he will inform the Captain of your insolence."

Jonnie and Bob exchanged funny looks and started to chuckle.

"The Cap'n isn't too pleased already," he said. "Come on, Jonathan, there's plenty of work ta be done on this old scow before we sail."

As he ducked into the hatchway, Jonnie followed right behind. His words hung on the now silent air and made me more than a little bit uneasy.

2

I looked up and could just see the sign over the top of the building: Four Anchors Hotel and Dining. The hotel was tall, four stories high, and built of red brick.

"Should we wait out here, Mother?" I asked meekly.

"NO!" she stated, much more loudly than I expected. "I mean, no dear, I think it would be best if you and your brother come inside with me. The weather is starting to blow up a bit."

I was reassured, although the weather didn't have anything to do with it. I didn't want to be left outside to take care of myself and Michael. I didn't feel comfortable with the people who were milling around. There were men, mostly sailors, strolling along the street, alone or in groups. They were too loud, and some were singing and Mother said she could smell alcohol on their breath as they walked by. There were also a few women, all dressed up as if they were going somewhere fancy, walking up and down the street as well. But, unlike the men, who seemed to want to be too friendly, the women crossed the street or looked away as we came close.

Mother pushed against the big revolving door of the hotel and Michael and I collided trying to get into the next compartment. We ended up in the same one and the door bumped heavily against my back foot. It almost came to a complete halt before it opened up into the lobby and we stumbled out.

"Stand," Mother ordered, pointing to a spot by a large potted plant beside the door.

There were big, dark paintings of ships at sea. The frames were heavy gold and stood out against the red velvet wallpaper. The carpeting was a rich royal blue but there was a worn-down path leading from the door to the counter. Above our heads hung a gigantic crystal chandelier. It was coated with dust. There was a damp smell in the air as if the whole place needed a good airing out. I suspected it was once something special. I could just imagine men and women in their Sunday finery, high tea and crumpets, bellhops in fancy uniforms and...

Rriiinnnggg!

I turned towards the sound. Mother was standing by a large oak counter, her hand suspended above a bell on the ledge. The ringing still echoed across the empty lobby. A few seconds later a door creaked open behind the counter and a man poked his head out.

"Yeah...can I help you?" he asked, scratching his head. He looked as if he'd just woken up, although it was only supper-time.

"Yes, I am here to speak to Mr. Stefansson."

"Have you checked the dining room?"

"We have checked nothing. Where would I find the dining room?"

He pointed to a set of tall, polished mahogany doors at the far side of the lobby. "Through there."

"Thank you," she replied curtly. She gestured for us to follow. She grabbed the tarnished brass handle and opened the door. We walked in behind her. Right inside the doors was a man in a faded uniform. Faded glory like the rest of the hotel.

"Seating for three?" he asked.

The dining room was almost as deserted as the lobby. There were people at only a few of the tables.

"No...no, thank you. I need to speak to Mr. Stefansson."

Before she'd even finished speaking, my eyes focused on a gentleman who I knew had to be him. He was sitting with three other men at a large table strewn with papers at the back of the dining room. They all seemed to be studying the papers intently. Stefansson, or at least the man I thought was him, had a neatly trimmed beard, short hair, a high-buttoned shirt and a fancy waistcoat. He looked like the sort of person who would ride all the time in a carriage like the kind we'd been in, or as if he was from a royal family, or a moving-picture star...or a character in one of my adventure stories.

Mother started walking towards their table, with Michael trailing behind. I followed. She came to a stop before them. The men continued to look at their papers, which I could now see were maps. They were concentrating so hard they didn't even notice us.

"Hhhhmmmmm," said Mother, clearing her throat. They all looked up.

"My name is Mrs. Kiruk and I am here to speak with Mr. Stefansson."

There was a scraping of chairs against the floor as first Mr. Stefansson, then the other men, rose to their feet. He towered above the others and was broad in the shoulders. From the pocket of his vest hung a long gold chain. He bowed slightly and extended his hand to Mother.

"I am Vilhjalmur Stefansson, and I am most pleased

to meet with you, Mrs. Kiruk," he said as they shook hands. He spoke with a gentle, lilting accent.

"As I am pleased to meet you," she replied.

"Could I invite you to sit with us? I will introduce you to these distinguished scientists who will be part of our expedition, but first, I would be honoured to be introduced to your children."

She introduced us by name. Mr. Stefansson offered Michael his hand and they shook. I did my best to curtsey, although I felt a little awkward.

"Mrs. Kiruk, you have such well-mannered children. And please do not find me too forward, but your daughter is going to be a striking young woman someday."

I felt my face redden and I looked down at the floor. Nobody had ever said such a thing to me before. I touched my hair to see if it was messy. It was bad enough it was always curling and twisting in ways I didn't want, but why did it have to be so mousy brown?

"Gentlemen, please get more chairs for these newest members of our expedition." Two men quickly brought over three chairs.

"You all must be tired and hungry and thirsty after your travels. I will order you a soft drink, or perhaps the children would prefer a dish of ice cream..." He paused. "Are you too old for ice cream, Helen?"

"No! I mean, no sir, I like ice cream. That is, if it's all right with you, Mother."

Both of us looked at her and pleaded with our eyes. Mother didn't believe in children being "indulged." She subtly nodded and we both burst into smiles. Stefansson motioned for the waiter, who came quickly to the table.

"I wish you to take my two special guests into your

cold storage and let them choose the flavour… and amount of ice cream that they wish," he said.

We got to our feet and followed the retreating waiter. He led us through a swinging door and into the kitchen. One man was standing beside a large stove and two women were seated at a counter, peeling and chopping vegetables.

"Who are your friends?" asked one of the women.

"Customers," the waiter corrected. "Guests of Mr. Stefansson."

He crossed the kitchen and pulled the handle on a large metal door. There was a metallic click and the door swung open. Frosty mist wafted into the warm air of the kitchen. He walked into the locker and motioned for us to enter. Stepping in, I was hit by a wave of cold and a shiver ran down my spine. The locker was lined with shelves filled with containers. There were a few dead chickens strung up by their feet and a whole side of beef on a big metal hook. The waiter reached up to a shelf, pulled down a large tub and plunked it on the wooden counter in the middle of the locker. "Vanilla." He reached up and grabbed a second tub. "Chocolate." He then took a third off the shelf and placed it beside the other two. "Strawberry, my favourite. I'll get you both a bowl," he said. As he walked towards the door, he stopped and gave us a big smile, "a big, big bowl."

"He's really something," I said.

"The waiter?" Michael asked.

"No, not the waiter… Mr. Stefansson."

"Stefansson? I guess so," Michael said as he dipped a finger into the strawberry tub. "Nobody ever offered me this much ice cream before."

"I don't mean the ice cream. I mean he's so… so… dashing," I replied and felt as though I was blushing again.

"Dashing?" Michael asked as he popped his finger into his mouth and licked off the ice cream. "Dashing …oh, dashing," he chuckled, and did a silly curtsey.

I was going to reach over and swat him when the waiter reappeared with two big bowls and a metal soup ladle. We pointed to our choices. He filled my bowl with chocolate and my brother's with strawberry. He led us out of the kitchen and back to Mother. We sat down and savoured our ice cream while the men and Mother continued to talk.

"Yes, Mrs. Kiruk, you are correct, our ship is not ideal," Stefansson noted.

"Far from it!" one of the other men agreed. "We need a ship like the *Flam*!"

"What's the *Flam*?" asked Michael between spoonfuls of ice cream.

"Michael! Listen but do not speak! Where are your manners?" reprimanded Mother.

"That is all right," Mr. Stefansson said quietly. "It is good he is confident enough to ask such questions. The *Flam* is a special ice ship. It has a very thick steel hull and its bottom is rounded so the ice cannot grasp it. It has recently completed a circumnavigation of the Arctic Ocean."

"I thought the Canadian government would have provided us with one of those new ice-breaker ships," added a third.

"Or at least something that wasn't so old," the fourth chipped in.

"How old is the ship?" asked Mother.

"Older than any of us!" chuckled one of the men.

"It is true she is neither young nor built for the ice, but as we speak she is being refitted to make her more suitable," Stefansson continued.

"We saw some men working when we dropped off our things. What are they doing?" Mother asked.

"Putting additional sheathing inside the hull and extra crossbeams to give the ship more strength," answered Stefansson.

"Good thing. That old ship would have cracked like a walnut the first time she hit ice!" said one of the men.

"Now, now…there is no need for such statements," Stefansson responded, turning directly to the man. "And it is not necessary to say things which might be of distress to the children." Stefansson now turned to Michael and me. "I want you both to know there is nothing to fear. We are being captained by one of the most qualified ice men in the world. He is the man who took Peary to the North Pole."

"To the North Pole!" Michael exclaimed.

I'd read a newspaper account of that journey. It was almost as exciting as my novels.

"Yes. Our captain is an interesting man…you would call him an old salt… He has more ice experience than any other man on the planet."

"I am very impressed you've secured such a man, Mr. Stefansson. Although, I must tell you I was not impressed with one member of the crew," said Mother.

Stefansson looked puzzled.

"One of the sailors working on the ship voiced his opinion, not very politely, that my children should not be accompanying me on this trip, and further, questioned your decision to allow this to take place."

"That is most, most unfortunate," Stefansson agreed. "Did you happen to learn his name?"

"Yes, I did. Bartlett, Bob Bartlett."

All at once there was an eruption of laughter which

quickly faded away. Mother's face mirrored my confusion.

"Please, Mrs. Kiruk, excuse our laughter, it is just… just that obviously you have already met our captain."

3

As we left the hotel, the winds were stronger and the skies dark.

"I will hail a coach for the journey," Mr. Stefansson announced. "We do not wish to be caught in the rain. Please wait here."

We stood under the canopy of the hotel while Mr. Stefansson hurried off. Within two or three minutes a carriage pulled to a stop and Mr. Stefansson emerged. I was a little disappointed. He'd hired a plain one instead of something as fancy as the one we'd ridden in earlier. The driver jumped off the top of the carriage and held open the door. Mr. Stefansson helped my mother climb in and then offered me his arm. I felt a little flustered and hoped the dim light would hide my blushing. Mother settled onto one bench facing forward and I sat opposite her. Michael came in next and sat down beside Mother, leaving a spot next to me for Mr. Stefansson. The carriage started moving.

"It was good of you to join our expedition on such short notice."

"That was not a problem, Mr. Stefansson."

"May I ask, did you have any trepidation about bringing your children on a two-year trip to the Arctic?"

"What's 'trepidation'?" Michael interrupted.

"It means worry or concern, Michael," Mother answered. "And I do have some concern. I still think it would have been better for them not to come, but circumstances dictated they accompany me."

"Circumstances?" asked Mr. Stefansson.

"Yes, there really isn't any close family to leave them with. And I had to keep my word. When my husband died, the children made me promise to never leave them."

"That's right, we're together," Michael added.

"A man's word…or a woman's word," Mr. Stefansson said, "must be their bond. It is good you brought them. They will be part of a wonderful adventure. Do you know what this venture is about, Michael and Helen?"

"Sort of…we're going up north to the Arctic."

"To the Arctic, yes. We are going to a place where very few people have ever been, and, this is my hope, to some places where no man has ever set foot."

"Wow! You mean nobody has ever been there?"

"I pray we are going to places no one even knows are there. That is why the Canadian government has sponsored an expedition of such large scale."

"How large is it to be, Mr. Stefansson? How many will be in our party?" Mother asked.

"Counting explorers, scientists, crew and natives, there are thirty-six members of our expedition."

"That's a lot of people," Michael said.

"It is a big country which we are to explore and discover and map. And, most important, our expedition must claim any new lands for the Dominion of Canada."

"I don't understand," I said. "I thought all of the north already belonged to our country."

"There are many people, many countries who would disagree with you, Helen. Explorers from Italy, Russia, the United States and Sweden are all mounting expeditions and would claim any new-found islands for their country."

"But I was taught in school all of the islands were the property of Britain, or the Hudson's Bay Company, and now they belong to Canada," I responded.

"You can only claim what you know. It is not enough to walk down a street and call out 'any money that is found belongs to me.' The money would belong to whoever finds it. Can you imagine being the first person to set foot on an island? It will be something you will tell your children and grandchildren that you were part of!"

"Children? I don't have any children. I'm only eleven years old," Michael replied in confusion.

"Michael, he means someday," I explained.

"Someday, no day. No way am I having kids 'cause there's no way I'm ever getting married!"

Mr. Stefansson reached over and put a hand on Michael's knee. "There are many reasons to marry…as well as many reasons not to marry."

"Are you married, Mr. Stefansson?" I blurted out, surprising myself, and from Mother's expression, her as well. I quickly looked away.

"No, Helen, I am not married. A man can only have one love in his life and mine is exploring. Besides it would not be fair to leave my wife behind for months or years at a time."

"Why couldn't you just bring her along?" asked Michael.

"The Arctic is a very wild and dangerous place, far too dangerous to bring along…" He stopped before completing his sentence, but I knew what he was going to say before he thought better of it.

He started again. "Helen, would you wish your husband to go off for months or years and go to bed each night wondering if he was still alive?"

"Ah...no, I guess not."

"You can see my reasons, yet for some the Arctic is well worth the dangers and discomforts. I am most pleased you and your brother agreed to make the journey with us."

"Ah...thank you," I answered, although the truth was I didn't want to be any part of this trip. I'd tried my best to talk Mother out of it. She explained to me that it was not something she wished to pursue either, but the money being offered would help to establish us when the trip was over. Even with Father, things had always been tough, but they'd been almost impossible since his death. I think the struggle and worry had worn away Mother's softness.

At that instant the carriage pulled to a stop, and I heard the driver leap to the ground. The door opened and Michael scrambled to his feet. Mr. Stefansson leaned forward, blocking him with his arm.

"Manners, Michael."

"Yes, sir," Michael answered, as he plopped down on his seat again.

Mother rose and the driver helped her disembark. I followed and again the driver offered his arm. Mr. Stefansson and then Michael emerged. We were standing on the road, in front of the dock. I shielded my face from the grit and dirt being blown about by the wind. Mr. Stefansson paid the driver and we proceeded down the pier. Up ahead I could see Jonnie, assisted by two other men, unloading a wagon alongside the ship. He waved to us and flashed me a big smile. I didn't know why, but I looked away and felt embarrassed.

"Please excuse me. I must attend to this matter. You should board and start to put your things in your cabin," said Mr. Stefansson.

We climbed down the ladder. As we reached the deck, the man we now knew was Captain Bartlett came up through the hatchway.

"Good day, Captain," Mother said.

"It'll be a good one when this ship is ready."

"I am sure that will be soon. Now, where would you like us to take our bags?"

"I'd like ya ta stow your gear back in town, but I don't think I'm goin' ta be gettin' what I like."

"Why do you object to us coming along?" Mother asked.

"This isn't some little fun trip. We're headed for the high Arctic!"

"I know our destination," replied Mother.

"Maybe ya do but ya don't know what that means. We're heading ta the most cold, desolate, inhospitable place in the world. This is the last place in the world a mother would want her children ta be."

"That is the place where I am going, so it is the place where my children will be going. Don't you think a mother's place is along with her children?"

"Course I do, in a snug, warm, safe house, waitin' for her man ta come home."

"There is no man to come home. The children's father, my husband, is dead."

Captain Bartlett looked taken aback for a second. "Sorry ta hear that, ma'am. But ya just don't understand what it's goin' to be like! I've seen grown men, big strong brave men, broke an' battered an'—"

"Those are my concerns, Mr. Bartlett!" interrupted Mother sharply.

"That's Cap'n Bartlett, and everything and everybody aboard this ship is my concern!" he snapped back.

"That is where you are wrong. I will take care of my children!"

"Then ya better get started," Bartlett said.

"What do you mean?"

"Up there," he answered, pointing up.

All eyes looked up. There, barely visible in the darkening sky, was Michael, climbing in the rigging, almost at the very top. I gasped.

"What now, Mrs. Kiruk?" asked Captain Bartlett.

Mother turned her eyes away from Michael and looked directly into Captain Bartlett's eyes. I knew how much she hated Michael's climbing. She had forbidden him to climb trees which were far shorter than the rigging to which he now clung.

"He climbed up, and he will climb down," she said calmly. "Now, where do you want us to put our bags?"

Captain Bartlett smiled slyly. "Follow me and I'll show ya ta your cabin."

"Thank you, Captain," she replied as he started to walk away. "And Captain?" He stopped and turned around. "It would be gentlemanly if you were to help carry some of our luggage."

"Maybe it would, but I'm neither a gentleman nor a babysitter…. I'm the Captain. Follow me if ya want ta know where you're goin' ta be stayin'," he said and disappeared down the hatch.

Mother started after him and I grabbed her arm. "What about Michael?" I asked.

"Leave him up there… for now. I'll tan his bottom when it finally reaches the deck. Wait here for him while I go below and see our quarters."

"Yes, ma'am."

I looked up at Michael scampering about like a squirrel. The winds were continuing to pick up, and I wished he'd come down soon. His climbing always made me anxious and I looked away. On the dock Jonnie and two other sailors were moving quickly. They were probably trying to outrace the coming storm. Little eddies of dust and dirt and papers swirled around, some being blown over the edge and into the water or onto the deck of the ship. Pieces of paper danced around my feet. I stamped my foot and trapped one. I bent down and picked up a torn piece of newsprint. I felt very much like this newspaper—blown about by uncontrollable forces.

4

July 18, 1913

Dear Diary,

    I'm sorry that it's been three days since my last entry, but I've been too sick to write anything. When the ship was tied up in the harbour I enjoyed the gentle rocking of the waves. But almost the instant we left port I felt myself getting seasick. I couldn't believe a ship this big could be picked up so high into the air and set back down again...and again...and again and again. Just writing this makes my stomach feel queasy again. Jonnie said it would take a little while for me to get my sea legs but it's my sea stomach I really want.

    Neither Mother nor my brother seem to be nearly as bothered by the motion as I am. My brother not being sick is even worse than being sick myself. He was like a little porcupine, needling me as I hung over the railing.

    We're sailing north, travelling what's called the inner island route, close to the shore and protected by islands from the open sea. What I can't believe, although Jonnie has told me it's true, is that the waves bashing us around aren't nearly as big as those on the open oceans.

I've had plenty of time to look at the scenery—tall trees that come almost right down to the water's edge, narrow stony beaches, rocky cliffs, inlets that twist away and disappear around bends, and high mountains in the distance draped in fog. Except for an occasional fishing boat, there's no sign of any other people.

Of course that doesn't mean there isn't any life. The skies are filled with birds of all kinds— some soaring overhead and vanishing into the horizon, while others seem to be following the ship as we sail. There are dolphins, dozens and dozens of them, escorting the ship, jumping and frolicking in the ship's wake. Twice the look-out has called out whale sightings but we never got close enough to see anything.

There are thirty-six people on board the ship. This includes the crew of the Karluk, the scientists, explorers, native guides and one passenger. The passenger, Mr. Hadley, is headed up north to set up a trading post. He's been very friendly towards us. All of them, with the exception of the Captain, have been pretty friendly and seem to like to explain things to us. Mr. Stefansson is very gallant. He is such a gentleman and so dashing and so…

I put down my pen and stopped writing. I didn't want to write anything I didn't want Michael to see because I knew sooner or later he'd get into my diary and poke fun at me. He'd already been teasing me about looking at Mr. Stefansson with "moon eyes."

I was careful not to write about my feelings. Although I was scared and worried, Mother didn't

want to hear about such thoughts. She wanted me to
"keep a stiff upper lip." I couldn't tell her how I was
feeling any more than I could allow her to hear me crying in my bed at night. She said she'd never seen a tear
solve a problem so there was no point in crying. I
hadn't seen her shed a tear since Father's funeral—or
laugh either. It was as though she'd buried her emotions
that day.

I turned back to my diary.

> Along with the people there are also ani-
> mals. There are fifty-four sled dogs on board. I
> was so excited when I found out we had dogs,
> but that excitement faded when I met them.
> They're more like wolves. They're called huskies
> and are trained only to pull sleds. They're
> always snapping and yelping at each other and
> getting into fights. The man who takes care of
> them (he's an Eskimo and I can't say his name or
> understand much of what he says) told us that
> one or two would be killed in these fights before
> we got to our base.
>
> There's also an old black-and-white cat. He
> seems a little skittish, like he's afraid of people.
> His name is Figaro, like the cat in Pinocchio.
> Captain Bartlett said to remember the cat has a
> job to do, catching mice and rats, and not to
> treat him as a pet. My mother, brother and I
> share a cabin and it's right next door to the Cap-
> tain's. A couple of times I've heard Figaro scrap-
> ing on the door of the Captain's cabin and I'm
> pretty sure that the Captain let him come in. I
> try to stay out of the Captain's way. He may be
> friendly to Figaro but he's hardly said two nice

words to me or my brother or Mother.

At first I wasn't pleased that our cabins were so close together. But I discovered one good thing about them being side by side. Lying in bed at night, over the sound of the waves and the creaking timbers, I can hear music. Jonnie told me Captain Bartlett has a gramophone in his cabin and what I hear are the records he plays. I love music almost as much as I love dogs.

The first night I heard the music, lying there in the dark of my cabin, I thought I was imagining things. Then, as I concentrated hard, I was able to make out more and more of the notes until I could figure out the melody. Now each night as I drift off to sleep I have one ear against the wall separating our cabins and the music vibrates inside my head.

I've learned a lot more about our expedition. We're sailing up the British Columbia coast, around Alaska and setting up our base on Herschel Island, just off the mouth of the Mackenzie River. The whole first winter everybody will stay there on the island and set up camp. Mr. Stefansson will lead a few trips across the ice. When the ice breaks up in the spring the Karluk will set off again and continue farther north and east. Maybe we'll go along with them but maybe we'll just stay on Herschel Island. I'll be happy to stay there on the island, but it does sound so romantic! Riding on the back of a dog sled...the cold winter winds blowing...discovering new land.

I stopped writing again. Of course, it's a lot less dangerous to read about adventures than to actually be in one. I knew I enjoyed reading about them. I just wasn't sure how I felt about taking part in one. The heroes in the stories never seem to be afraid, but I've been frightened ever since Mother first told us what we were going to do.

In fact, I don't remember not being afraid since Father died. Life used to be good—going to school with my friends, playing with Michael, Father coming home from work and sweeping me up in his arms, the four of us sitting around the kitchen table eating meals, Mother tucking me into bed and singing me a lullaby before kissing me good night. And then it all changed.

5

"Helen, get your nose out of that book or you'll miss it!" Michael shouted as he bounded into the room.

"Miss what?" I asked, peering over the top of the book.

"Hurry up. Come up on deck and you'll see!"

"Nothing could be more exciting than what's in my novel," I said, tapping the cover of one of my very favourite books.

"I don't understand you at all," Michael replied. "The way you act sometimes, it's like those characters in the books are real and the rest of us are just made-up people." Maybe not more real but certainly more interesting, I thought, but didn't answer. "Besides, doing almost anything is better than reading about something. Come on up top or you'll miss it."

"But—"

"But nothing, Helen. I'll meet you on deck."

He was gone before I could raise any more objections. Maybe he was right, but I knew for sure it was definitely warmer in my cabin. The temperature was dropping so quickly as we sailed north that nothing but my heaviest winter dresses kept away the cold.

Regardless, I thought it best to go topside. I'd been in the cabin all morning, not even venturing out as far as the kitchen for breakfast, and I knew Mother would be cross with me for "lazing about" if I didn't at least get a breath of fresh air. I started to leave, but turned back to put on another sweater to ward off the chill.

Stepping through the hatch to the deck I was shocked to see a thin film of snow covering everything. I bent down to touch it and something whizzed by my head and smashed against the wall behind me. A snowball! I looked up and saw Michael standing by the rail of the ship, a guilty smile on his face.

"You're lucky I missed," he said.

"Not as lucky as you were," I replied threateningly. "So what's so exciting?"

"We just crossed over."

"Crossed over what?"

"The Circle. The Arctic Circle!" Michael exclaimed. "We're in the Arctic!"

"That would explain the snow."

"Not quite," came a gravelly voice from behind me. I turned around to see Captain Bartlett. "Snow this early, this far south isn't usual...or good."

"But...but...doesn't it always snow in the Arctic?" Michael stammered. He must have been as surprised as me to have the Captain talking to us, and it took a little while for him to find his tongue.

"Arctic doesn't get much snow...'specially in August."

"A little snow doesn't matter, does it?" I asked timidly.

"No, but what it means does matter. Air's cold, cold before its time. Could mean an early freeze-up."

"How long before we get to Herschel Island?" I asked.

"Maybe six days, but could be as many as ten, dependin'..."

"Depending on what?"

"Wind at our back, water stays clear of ice."

"Ice! There won't be ice yet, will there?"

"No tellin'. Seen some floes already, but we can sail around 'em, as long as we don't get a freeze-up."

"It wouldn't freeze up, would it?" asked Michael.

"Could...just hope it won't." He turned and walked away, disappearing behind one of the bulkheads.

"That was almost friendly," Michael noted, "or at least friendly for him."

"I guess. Do you think he was kidding about the ice floes?"

"I don't know. Let's go and ask Jonnie," suggested Michael. My brother turned and walked away and I hurried after him.

It wouldn't be hard to find Jonnie. If he wasn't on deck working he could always be found in the kitchen, sitting at the big galley table sipping hot coffee and gabbing with the cook. They were both from the same little outport on the Newfoundland coast. I'd also found out that Captain Bartlett was from Newfoundland, but from a much bigger village. We burst into the kitchen and found Jonnie, as expected.

"Mornin'!" he said cheerfully, rising to his feet. "How's your first breath of good Arctic air feel?"

"About the same, only colder," Michael responded.

Jonnie came over and pulled out a chair for me. I sat down and Michael took the empty seat beside me. Without being asked, the cook set down two bowls of steaming oatmeal in front of us. There was always a big pot of something simmering on the stove.

"I ain't been seein' ya about much, Helen. Ya gettin' yer sea legs?"

"I'm feeling much better, thank you for asking. I just like to spend time reading."

Actually it had been a challenge even to read with my stomach being so unsettled.

"She spends her life reading," added Michael.

"I have many fine books," I said proudly, "if ever you want to borrow one."

"Thank ya. I might drop on by an' take a peek at your books, but I ain't got much time ta be readin', what with all the work ta be done."

"Surely there must be some time for you to..." I stopped short. Jonnie was gazing down at his coffee mug. I remembered how he said he'd only gone to fourth form and I wondered if he could read very well. I hadn't meant to embarrass him.

"Jonnie, the Captain was telling Michael and me about ice floes."

"Seen a couple," he answered, getting up to refill his coffee cup.

"Big ones?" I asked apprehensively.

"A few, but nothin' ya needs ta be worried none 'bout."

I think he could tell by the look on my face I wasn't particularly reassured.

"I been sealin' with the Cap'n up near Greenland last winter. The floes was so big an' close tagether ya wouldn't 'ave thunk ya could 'ave got a rowboat between 'em... but he done it. Many's the time we 'ad ta use pry bars ta make a space big enough ta let the ship on through."

"That sounds frightening."

"It was. Big bergs get calved off from the glaciers an' come sailin' on down. Some of 'em higher than the top of the mast. Ya just pray they don't come splintering down on top of ya."

"Wow!" exclaimed Michael.

"We won't be seein' no floes like that up here. 'Sides, up in Greenland the Cap'n would be tryin' to get close ta the floes."

"Why would he want to do that?" I asked in amazement.

"'Cause that's where the seals is...on the ice...if ya can't get close ya can't catch 'em." Jonnie looked at me and I think he could tell none of this was making me feel any better.

"The Cap'n will be steering us wide of any ice he can. You don't 'ave ta worry none about any ice floes."

"So we have nothing to worry about?"

"Didn't say that. Just said ya didn't have ta worry about floes."

"Then what should we worry about?" I asked.

"Freeze-up."

"Freeze-up?"

"Solid ice. Can't steer around it, can't get through it. We'd be trapped."

6

I awoke with a start and sat up in bed. The cabin was completely dark and I felt warm and snug inside my sleeping sack. Mother has been working feverishly to make one for everybody. She sews two thick blankets together and adds a layer of caribou skins on the outside. The skins are rough to the touch but are very warm. Only the top is open where your head sticks out and the other three sides are sewn together.

The hides came from the hold. I was down there a few times to get things for Mother. It's filled with supplies the expedition will need for the entire two-year trip. It's brimming with wooden boxes, stacks of canned goods, bushels of potatoes and apples, wood, tents, blankets and lots more. It reminds me of a general store, except there isn't rock candy in a glass container on a counter.

The cabin was completely silent, except for the faint sound of breathing from my brother and Mother sleeping. Nothing to worry about.

Then it struck me: there was no other sound. Over the past few days there'd been the constant sound of the ship crunching through the skin of ice covering the sea. The ice wasn't thick, but breaking through made a constant sound: a grating, grinding, snapping noise, almost like the sound sugar makes underfoot when you accidentally drop some on the floor and then walk on it. And now it was gone. We must have hit open water.

I lay back in my bed and breathed a big sigh of relief. Everything was going to be okay. Then as quickly as my sense of relief came, it was gone. I had a premonition something wasn't right. I couldn't instantly put my finger on it, but I knew something was wrong …something was missing…it was as if we weren't moving. I held my breath and tried to lie completely motionless. I concentrated and tried to feel something, anything, any hint of the waves rocking the ship. The rhythm of the ship, up and down and side to side, was gone. The ship wasn't moving!

I drew my legs up and wiggled out of the sleeping sack. I was still dressed in my night clothes and the chill of the cabin instantly seeped through the material. I threw my legs over the side of the bunk and located my shoes. I tied them up quickly. As I stood up, I stumbled and fell back to the bed. The floor was locked on an angle. The ship was frozen in place.

Carefully I rose to my feet again, holding on to the bed with one hand. Quietly, so as not to disturb my mother, I slipped my coat on over my night clothes. I moved across the cabin, opened the door and went into the corridor, silently closing the door behind me.

I could see my breath in the faint glow thrown by an oil lamp hanging at the far end of the walkway. At the hatchway the light became brighter, not just from the lamp but from the sunlight coming in from above. Even though it was late, and I wasn't sure how late, the sun would still be in the sky until the middle of the "night." Jonnie told me that during June and part of July the sun stayed up in the sky all night long, sort of like a day that lasted eight weeks. Michael liked that. He said if

Mother told him to come in when it got dark, he could stay out and play for two more months.

Opening the hatch I was struck by both the cold and the eerie "midnight sun." I stepped out onto the deck. There was a strange silence. Not even the wind was breathing. Then I heard voices. I walked around the bulkhead and saw a group of men standing by the rail talking. Jonnie was among them, listening but not really part of the discussion. He saw me and walked over.

"Little late, ain't it, Helen?"

"I guess so. What time is it?"

He pulled out a watch hanging on the end of a chain and opened it up. "Quarter past one."

I nodded. "We're frozen in, aren't we?"

It was Jonnie's turn to nod.

"How bad is it?"

"Come an' 'ave a look," Jonnie said, motioning me to follow him to the side of the ship.

Looking out, I was taken aback by the view. As far as the eye could see, all the way to the horizon, the sea was a solid mass of shimmering ice. I could make out a series of ripples and bumps and ridges that marred the surface, but there was no hint of the water underneath.

"Pretty thick…too thick ta break through. Cap'n's sending out a party in the morning ta check 'ow far it goes. I t'ink it's over a mile ta open water…too far ta cut through I t'ink."

"Nobody pays ya ta think, Jonathan," came the Captain's voice from behind me.

I turned to face him.

"Jonathan, ya better get below deck an' grab some rest. You'll be needin' your energy fer tomorrow…when we may have ta cut our way through." Instantly Jonnie turned and headed for the hatch.

"Cut our way through?" I repeated, not quite sure what he meant.

"Ya questionin' my orders too?"

"No sir!...I just didn't understand what you meant ...that was all, sir," I apologized.

"It means what I said. We'll be gettin' out the long saws an' cuttin' out a place for the ship ta slip through."

"But Jonnie said it was over a mile."

"Maybe, maybe not. A mile or two we can cut through," he answered.

"And if it's farther than that?" I asked, afraid of what his answer might be.

"Then we don't cut through."

"What do we do then?"

"Nothin'," he answered.

"Nothing?"

"Nothin'. We just sit an' wait an' pray it warms up some or the winds shift an' a path opens up."

"So all of those things could happen, right?" I asked hopefully.

"Could. Lots of things could happen. But probably won't."

"You mean that..." I couldn't bring myself to finish the sentence. My heart suddenly felt as cold as the ice surrounding the ship.

Captain Bartlett nodded. "Something my gramma used ta say ta me when I was about your age: 'Pray for the best, an' prepare for the worst.' So...I want ya ta do just that...go down below, lass, get inta your bed and say a prayer."

7

I went back to bed but was able to catch only short snatches of sleep. I waited anxiously until Michael started moving in his bed and I knew he was awake. I tiptoed across the cabin and told him what had happened. We didn't want to disturb Mother, so we dressed quietly and hurried up onto deck.

Huddled together in small groups were members of the expedition. Some were bundled in the new coats Mother had made. She had been working almost nonstop the last week to outfit everybody for the cold which had come so much sooner than predicted. The sun was now much brighter, although the air was chilly and a stiff breeze was blowing so hard it cut right through my old coat. I hadn't gotten one of the new ones yet. Mother had said it wouldn't look right for me or Michael or her to have new coats until she'd made them for everybody else. Jonnie had offered to let me use his new one until mine was ready, but I'd turned him down. It was better to be cold than have my brother tease me any more about Jonnie being sweet on me.

"I hear dogs, but I can't see them," Michael said.

I ran over to the starboard railing. Down on the ice two teams of dogs stood, hooked up to sleds. Their Eskimo handler was crouched over on the ice and three members of the expedition were standing just off to one side.

Michael came up beside me. "It's like a giant skating rink."

"Search party off the starboard!" yelled out a voice.

I turned and looked up. It was the lookout, up in the crow's nest at the top of the front mast. My eyes turned back to the ice and I scanned the horizon. The glare off the ice was so strong I had to cup my hands over my eyes.

At first I couldn't see anything. Then I started to make out a small, dark shape on the very edge of the horizon. I strained my eyes to see what it was.

"Comin' down?" asked Jonnie.

"Down where?"

"Ta the ice. We's goin' down on the ice."

"Sure!" Michael said, breaking my concentration.

"Shouldn't we stay here?"

"You can stay here. I'm going down," Michael replied.

The men began moving aft. Reluctantly I followed the crowd. At the rear of the ship was a ladder leading down. One after another the men filed down the ladder and took to the ice. Michael was the last one, leaving me alone on deck. I hesitated for a moment and stared back out at the incoming figures. It looked like two teams of dogs. I took a deep breath to steady my nerves and started down the ladder. At the bottom I tentatively placed one foot on the ice. I knew, having seen all those men and dogs on the ice, that it would hold me, but I still felt nervous. I put all my weight on the ice. It was solid and smooth, rippled with cracks and bubbles beneath the surface. Carefully, making sure my feet didn't slide out from under me, I moved over to where everyone stood. There was a feeling of anticipation. People were talking, and even the dogs seemed to be getting excited, probably sensing or smelling the in-coming teams.

Michael was standing beside the dog handler, whose name was Kataktovick. It was hard to tell how old he was, his face was so worn and weathered. He had jet black hair and wasn't much taller than me. He didn't speak very much English, but this hadn't stopped my brother from spending time with him by the pens where the dogs were kept. Michael was teaching him some English, and Kataktovick was teaching Michael things about the animals. The most important thing that he'd learned, at least that he'd told me, was how some dogs were nice and some were pretty mean. Michael said he now knew which dogs to avoid. Of course, this hadn't stopped him from getting bitten. It wasn't a bad bite, and Dr. Mackay had fixed it up. I didn't find out about it until two days later, when he was getting changed. He made me promise not to tell Mother.

The two sleds were now so close I could make out the men driving the teams. I wasn't surprised. One sled was being driven by Mr. Stefansson and his assistant, Burt McConnell. On the other team was one of the Eskimos, whose name I couldn't remember, and Cap-tain Bartlett. Side by side the two teams came towards us. They stopped in our midst. Kataktovick stood up, followed by Michael, and walked over to them.

"Well, Cap'n?" said Alex Anderson. Mr. Anderson was the ship's first mate.

"Not so well," Captain Bartlett answered. "Solid ice, for close ta two miles in all directions. We're smack in the middle of this pan of ice. Then there's some open water an' fresh leads...places where the ice has just frozen an' it can't support a man or dog."

"Is there any way out?" asked one of the scientists,

Mr. Diamond Jenness.

"Or off?" asked another.

"None I know of," Bartlett answered. "Too far an' too thick ta cut our way through an' not solid enough ta sled our way off."

"There must be some way!" somebody protested.

"I am afraid there is not," Mr. Stefansson interrupted. "The Captain is correct. There is nothing that we can do at this time."

"We can't just sit here! We're only a two-day sled ride from Herschel Island," objected Mr. Jenness. He was an anthropologist and was on this expedition to study the natives in the area.

"I wish we were just sittin' here," Captain Bartlett replied.

"What do you mean?"

"We're movin', right now, as we talk. This pan of ice is floating at about eight knots."

"In which direction?"

"South-west...away from Herschel Island an' ta-wards the coast of Alaska," answered Bartlett.

"Then we must leave immediately!" Jenness said loudly. "Even worse than sitting here, we're moving farther and farther from our goal!"

"You can go if ya want...although I think maybe you're missin' a couple of things that would make it possible."

"What do you mean? What am I missing?" asked Jenness angrily.

"Feathers an' wings. Only way off this pan is ta fly."

"Very amusing, Captain," Jenness answered, although I could tell he was far from amused.

Bartlett walked past Jenness and towards the ship. Jenness reached out and grabbed the Captain by the shoulder, spinning him around. Bartlett looked at the hand on his shoulder and then fixed his eyes directly on Jenness.

"I'm goin' 'board ship for a cup of java. Ya can join me, or..." he let the sentence trail off. Mr. Jenness removed his hand from Bartlett's shoulder.

8

Dear Diary,

This has been the longest five weeks of my life. Each day seems even longer than the one before. Everybody except my brother and I have something they have to be doing. Every morning parties of men go out on the sleds and scout for a break in the ice—something they can cut a passage towards. The water under the ice, the current, keeps moving and it causes the ice to shift and buckle and grind, making ominous sounds. Sometimes places open up, or press together into ridges that rise high up into the sky. When it buckles, they have to take their pick-axes and hack a trail right through it. In the places where it opens up it quickly freezes again. These are called fresh leads and you don't know you're on one until you fall through the thinner ice. I heard Captain Bartlett say he can tell a new lead by the colour of the ice; it looks a little more blue and a little less white. So far we've had two men and a few dogs fall through. It was scary to see somebody go into the water. I saw it happen just a hundred yards off the port side of the ship. I was watching one of the scientists walking towards the ship and then he just dropped down through the ice. They got him out quickly and he was all right but it frightened me so much I didn't venture onto the ice again for almost a week. Not that I ever went far from the ship. The only time I left was with Jonnie each morning when he went out to measure the depth of the ice. And each day the ice grows thicker.

Mr. Stefansson told me this was the most dangerous time of year to be travelling on the ice. Later, when it's much thicker, there's less chance of falling through to the freezing water below.

Mother is working almost non-stop and hardly has time to even say good morning or good night. Why did she even bring us along if she was going to be so busy she doesn't even spend a moment with us?

Two of the Eskimos have been helping her design and work on the clothing. Together they've almost finished making everybody's winter outfits: hooded parka, pants, big mitts and boots like those worn by the Eskimos, called mukluks. She had me try on the boots she was making for me. I couldn't believe how big they were! I could almost put both feet into one boot. When I told her they couldn't possibly be for me, she said she was told to make them big so we could wear many extra socks to keep warm. I couldn't even imagine ever needing that many pairs of socks to keep warm.

It's been very hard for Mother because the clothes are made from animal skins and they're very tough. She's broken off many needles and *her hands are getting all calloused.*

Mr. Stefansson says Mother has the most important job on the whole expedition. If people aren't dressed in warm clothes, clothes that will keep a body warm and protect them from the wind and even be waterproof, then they'll die. I've heard all sorts of tales about people getting frostbite so badly they lose fingers or toes or even their feet. I think that would be so awful and...

My thoughts drifted back to our warm safe house... I guess it really wasn't our house any more...somebody else was living there now...somebody with enough money...

"Helen, stop writing and come and see the morning parties off," Michael ordered as he opened the cabin door.

I put my pen down, although I wasn't writing when he barged in. "What's to see? They've been going off and coming back every morning."

"I don't know, but from the way they're loading up the sleds I think they might be going a lot farther today."

"Farther?"

"I heard a couple of the men say they might even be heading for land if they can find ice to support them."

None of this was news to me. There'd been talk of parties leaving the ship since almost the first day we'd been locked in, but it never amounted to anything.

"What makes you think today will be any different?"

"I heard we've drifted closer to land and the ice may be solid right to shore. Besides the ice is getting thicker all the time. Why not today?"

What he said made sense. "Who's going, and how many are—" Before I could finish my sentence Michael retreated out of the cabin. He was probably headed back to the deck. I walked over to the tall locker and placed the open diary on top. I didn't want my brother to read it, but I couldn't close and lock it until the ink had dried. Luckily the locker was so tall the diary was out of sight and Michael hadn't discovered my hiding place. I screwed the lid back on the bottle of ink. With the cabin getting colder by the day the ink was becoming much thicker and more difficult to write with.

I retreated to my bedside and put on my boots. I wanted Mother to finish my mukluks as soon as possible. It would be more awkward to move around but I wanted to get used to wearing them.

I reached down and adjusted the leggings I wore under my skirt. Even my longest and heaviest dress wasn't warm enough without the leggings underneath. Next I pulled on a heavy sweater, and hurried out of the cabin. Then I remembered my mittens and ran back for them. I was always forgetting them, but I knew it was important to have them with me.

Usually when the sun was out it was warm enough, but when the sun went down it got chilly very fast. The sun was now setting at four in the afternoon. With no trees or buildings or hills to slow down the wind it just whipped across the ice, picking up speed and cold.

Coming onto the deck I wasn't surprised to see that nobody was there. I knew they'd all be down on the ice. The deck was littered with boxes and cannisters and barrels. Things which had been stowed away below were being brought up top. At first this didn't make much sense to me. The crew complained, to themselves, about having to lug everything up, but they followed the Captain's orders. My mother said she thought he was just trying to keep people busy, keep their minds off being trapped, but I didn't think so. There was too much order to what they were bringing up. They weren't just carrying whatever was closest to the hatches but specific things Captain Bartlett ordered: kerosene, coal, gasoline, water and food. All the things you'd need to feed a fire or a person.

I walked aft. The dog pens were empty. All the animals were now living on the ice. The ladder leading down had been replaced by a crude set of stairs made from discarded crates. Below me were four shelters constructed out of slabs of ice and snow. They were dome-shaped and called "igloos." The two largest were for the dogs, although most of the time they were staked in the open. They were happier on the ice than on board ship, and from what Kataktovick had told Michael, healthier as well. Kataktovick and the other Eskimos lived in the other two shelters. The shelters were all the same shape, with a roof that curved right over the top. They almost looked like big white beehives.

Michael and I had been inside them. You had to get right down on your belly and crawl up a sloping tunnel to enter. Inside it was much warmer than on the ice. Michael had asked if he could spend the night in one with Kataktovick. At first Mother had agreed, but then she heard about the polar bear tracks that had been discovered right through the middle of the little huddle of ice shelters. The bear had wandered through, without bothering anything, or anybody even noticing it.

Mr. Hadley said polar bears aren't like other wild animals that will usually run or shy away from people. They haven't seen enough people to be afraid of them.

To a polar bear a person is no different from a seal or a salmon—just another meal. Mother said she hadn't raised her son to be bear food.

What I'd heard, sitting around the big table in the galley, and something Mother didn't know, was that the danger in the ice huts didn't come from bears, but from the ice. There was no telling where a pressure ridge would form, or where the ice might just crack. It could open up right under where you were sleeping, plunging you into the freezing water below, catching you in the current, pulling you down below the surface, your raised hand disappearing below the freezing water, weighed down by all the heavy clothing, the air forced out of your lungs, and…I shuddered. I didn't ever put my foot onto the ice without thinking about what might happen. At least having Jonnie close by when I was down there made me feel safer.

It was obvious, even to me, that the sleds were being prepared for a longer expedition. They were piled high with food and gear and supplies. Both sleds had seven dogs hooked up. I'd gotten to know the snarling, yelping pack of huskies well enough to know that these fourteen dogs were amongst the biggest and strongest.

Standing by one sled was Burt McConnell and one of the Eskimo hunters. Beside the other sled were three men—one of the other Eskimos, and George, who was the trip's photographer, and Mr. Jenness. I wouldn't be sad to see Mr. Jenness go. He made me even more nervous than the Captain. He had hard piercing eyes and never seemed to have time to talk to anybody. I knew the sixth member of the expedition would be Mr. Stefansson. He led almost every trip away from the ship. Mother said men like Mr. Stefansson are never very good at waiting. They didn't understand that "patience is a virtue." I knew, from sitting in the galley and listening to him talk, he didn't have time to be patient. While we were locked into the ice, he was worried other explorers could be working their way towards the discoveries that "belonged" to him.

I loved sitting in the galley, sipping on a hot chocolate and drinking in stories. Mr. Stefansson was a wonderful storyteller. He told us all about his adventures, other explorers and even fairy tales. Listening to him talk I could feel a warm glow in my head and sometimes I'd just close my eyes and try to see it all in my mind.

It wasn't just Mr. Stefansson, though, who told stories. Almost everybody sitting around the table took turns. I was shocked one day when Michael started telling a tale about how the spirits created the polar bear from snow and ice. It was a wonderful story. Later I asked him about it and he said it was a story told by one of the Eskimos; Mr. Hadley had translated it. He said that since they didn't write anything down they had stories for everything.

Being in the galley, surrounded by all those men, reminded me of the times Father would be working late and I'd take a meal up to the mine for him. All the miners would be sitting together, eating and talking before heading back down into the pit. Mother was always hesitant about me going up there, because she said the tone wasn't appropriate for a young girl. But there were many days when this was the only way I could see him and Mother knew how much I missed him…how much I miss him.

Turning around I saw Mr. Stefansson, and then Captain Bartlett, emerge from one of the ice shelters. Mr. Stefansson walked through the crowd. He moved

so regally, his head up and his chest out. The Captain
shuffled along behind him. Mr. Stefansson came to one
of the sleds and stepped up on it so he was head and
shoulders above the people gathered around. It looked
as though everybody, with the exception of Mother
working below deck and the cook preparing breakfast
in the galley, was gathered on the ice.

"Could I have your attention!" he called out.

Everyone fell silent. Even the dogs stopped yapping,
as if they too were interested in his words.

"Gentlemen," he started, then paused and looked
directly at me, "and lady." He gave me a big smile and
I blushed and looked down at the ice. "I will be leading
a party which will travel farther from the ship than any
of our previous trips. It is my hope we will make the
land which was within sight of yesterday's exploration
party. If successful we will mark a trail to shore, and
return with fresh meat from the caribou herds. We will
be gone for at least three days. In my absence, Captain
Bartlett will be in charge of not only the *Karluk* but the
entire expedition." He gestured to the Captain, who
stood on the ice beside him. "We must leave with the
light, but I promise you all upon our return fresh caribou, the greatest delicacy known to man."

A cheer went up from the huddle of men. The dogs
joined with their own chorus of approval. Mr. Stefansson waved his arms in the air and then disappeared
from my view, hidden behind the other men, as he
stepped down from the sled. Almost instantly the sleds
started moving and the group of men fanned out as
they watched them start off. I moved over to stand
beside Michael. I followed them with my eyes as they
moved along "Main Street," a flat, clean, clear patch of
ice stretching away from the ship. Distances were

deceiving on the ice, but this trail went on for over a mile until it reached a pressure ridge which had risen up twenty feet into the air. A passage, just wide enough for a sled to pass, had been hacked through the ridge.

Slowly people turned away and started wandering back to the ship, climbing the stairs to leave the ice. I stood and watched as the teams became smaller and smaller on the horizon. Finally even the sounds of the dogs didn't come back to my ears. I observed them until finally they reached the icy ridge, and first one sled, and then the other, went through the passage and disappeared from view.

"HELEN! MICHAEL!" sang out Mother's voice. She was standing on the ship, peering over the railing. She had yet to leave the ship. We both walked over until we stood directly below her. I wondered if she'd seen all of what had just gone on.

"Have you both had breakfast?" she asked.

"No, ma'am," I answered.

"Michael?"

"Not yet...but I'm not hungry."

"I want you both to come and eat right now."

"But Mom, I have to help feed the dogs," Michael protested.

"The dogs can wait. I want you to eat breakfast right now."

"But Mother!" Michael started to protest before he was cut short.

"Don't 'but' me, young man. There may be no trees for me to cut a switch but I can still warm your behind! Do you understand?"

"Yes, ma'am," he answered quietly, looking down at his feet.

"Good. I'm going to have breakfast myself," she

said and walked out of our view.

Her words brought an instant smile to my face. This would be one of the few times in weeks we'd eaten with Mother. She'd been taking her meals alongside her sewing machine.

"Come on, Michael."

"I'm going to eat breakfast with Kataktovick."

"But Mother said to—" I started.

"Eat breakfast," he interrupted, "and that's what I'm going to do. I'm just not going to eat in the galley."

"Mother will be very angry!" I warned him, but I doubted he'd take either my words or her threat very seriously. He started to walk away.

"Michael!" I called out.

He turned around. He looked like he was ready for an argument.

"Tell Kataktovick I'll be down to see the dogs later."

Michael smiled. "I'll tell him." He walked away towards one of the igloos, while I went around the side of the ship.

As I walked, I removed one glove and reached into one of the pockets of my parka. I felt a couple of small pieces of meat nestled there. I always kept a couple of scraps for one of the dogs, Daisy, who was much gentler than the other dogs. She always made a fuss and licked my hands. She'd learned I had treats for her and would push her muzzle against me as she tried to figure out which pocket it was in. I decided to go down and see her right after breakfast.

I climbed the stairs two at a time and then hurried below deck to the galley. Mother was already seated at the big table, as were Dr. Mackay, Mr. Hadley and Captain Bartlett. There was an empty seat on each side of Mother. I gave her a small kiss on the cheek before sitting down beside her.

"Where is your brother?"

"He's having breakfast…with Kataktovick…on the ice."

"He is what?" she demanded.

"Having breakfast with Kataktovick," I repeated quietly.

"I heard what you said! I meant, why isn't he here? He knew perfectly well what I meant."

"Just what the boy needs, a breakfast of blubber," Mr. Hadley laughed.

"Blubber?" I asked.

"Yeah, raw whale or seal fat…that's what those people eat, you know," he explained.

"Blubber! He can't eat blubber for breakfast!" Mother said, turning white. "Helen, you go and get your brother immediately!"

Before I could even take to my feet, Captain Bartlett spoke. "They eat a lot more than blubber, Mrs. Kiruk. Lots of things. 'Member these people live up here an' they know what they should be eatin'. If Michael eats like a native he'll stay healthy like 'em. Isn't that right, Doc?"

The doctor put down his steaming cup of coffee. "The natives do seem to handle these barbaric living conditions remarkably well. Although, I must admit I've never actually treated or examined one."

"Good thing you haven't," Mr. Hadley chipped in. "If you've ever had to be at close quarters with one of them you'd realize they stink to the high heavens! Dirty, filthy Indians is what they are."

"They aren't dirty. It just don't make sense to bathe up here unless ya want ta die of pneumonia," noted Captain Bartlett.

"Well, as my dear departed mother used to say, 'cleanliness is next to Godliness,' and these people don't have any of either. Nothing but heathens. Godless, dirty Indians, the whole bunch of them."

"They have their God," Captain Bartlett said.

"What do you mean by 'their God'? Last time I was in church the minister told me there was only one God. I have yet to meet an Eskimo who was a Christian."

"Inuit," Captain Bartlett said.

"In your what?" asked Mr. Hadley.

"Inuit ... not Eskimos or Indians. They call themselves Inuit. It means 'the people.'"

"They aren't my people. Now if you'll excuse me," Mr. Hadley said, rising from his seat. "There's no point in you and I discussing this again, Robert. I don't know why you have such a soft spot for these Indians, so I'll not waste my time. I have things to attend to."

As he opened the door to leave, Michael walked in and took a seat.

"I thought you were eating elsewhere," Mother commented.

"Changed my mind when I saw the menu. Raw fish and some other stuff that was all dried out. It looked like shoe leather."

Cookie put down a big bowl of porridge in front of Michael, who instantly dug into it. He swallowed a big mouthful. "This is good, but I can't wait to taste caribou."

"You'll have to wait," the Captain said.

"I guess so. Mr. Stefansson said he wouldn't be back for at least a few days."

Captain Bartlett rose from the table, carrying his empty bowl and ever-present coffee mug. He walked over and placed the bowl in the sink and then refilled his mug from the steaming urn.

"I don't want ya ta be disappointed, Michael. Remember he's not goin' ta the general store ta pick up some grub. This is the Arctic. Maybe he can't find caribou. Maybe he hits bad weather and gets socked in. Maybe the ice breaks up and he can't get back ta the ship."

"Can't get back to the ship!" I exclaimed. "But if he can't get back to the ship then he'll…" I bit down hard on my lower lip to stop the tears which suddenly threatened to erupt.

"Vilhjalmur knows more about the Arctic than almost any man alive. 'Sides, he has good men, good dogs an' plenty of supplies along with him," Captain Bartlett said. "He'll be just fine an' dandy."

"Thank you, Captain, that is very nice of you to reassure Helen," said Mother.

"Not tryin' ta be nice, ma'am. Just tellin' facts as I see 'em. Vilhjalmur will do just fine. No sense in worryin'…leastways about him. We have too much ta do ta waste time worryin'."

"What still needs to be done?" asked Dr. Mackay.

Captain Bartlett turned directly to Mother. "Clothes all done?"

"Yes, as of yesterday."

"Good, 'cause I'm goin' ta need your help ta construct the komatiks."

"What is a ko…ma…tik?"

"Here, let me show ya," Captain Bartlett said. He pulled out a piece of paper from the pocket of his jacket. He unfolded it and flattened the paper on the table in front of Mother. Both Michael and I peered at the rough pencil drawing.

"It looks like a sled," observed Michael.

"Special type of sled...a type used by the Inuit. Kataktovick helped me with the drawing."

"Why do we need new sleds?" asked Dr. Mackay.

"The ones we have are too big an' bulky."

"I've been out on a few trips, Robert, and they seem to work just fine," Dr. Mackay disagreed.

"Fine for little trips, but not for anything longer. 'Sides, we don't have enough sleds for what we'll be needin'."

"What are these made of?" asked Mother, pointing to the picture.

"Wooden frames covered by seal an' caribou skins, mostly. I'll make sure the frames are made an' then help ya ta stretch the skins atop 'em."

"What else needs to be done?" Dr. Mackay asked.

"Have to finish what we started. All the rest of the supplies have ta be brought up on deck. Some should even be taken down onta the ice."

"The ice! Why in good God would we need to do that?"

"Like my gramma always said, 'don't put all your eggs in one basket,'" Captain Bartlett replied.

Dr. Mackay's face took on a serious look. "These are very troubling suggestions, Robert. From what you're saying I can only assume you think that the ship is in..."

Captain Bartlett stood up and placed a hand on the doctor's shoulder. "Helen an' Michael, could ya go an' find Jonathan for me? Tell him I need ta see him."

"Could I finish my porridge first, sir?" asked Michael.

"No! Go with your sister right now!" Mother insisted.

Both Michael and I recognized that tone and we

instantly rose to our feet and hurried out of the galley. The door swung shut behind us.

"First she orders me to come and eat and when I try to eat she orders me to leave. That doesn't make any sense. I wonder what's so all-fired important they need to talk to Jonnie?" complained Michael.

"They didn't send us away just to find Jonnie. They wanted to..." I started and then stopped, realizing Michael didn't have any idea why we were sent away. There was no point in worrying him too. At least one of us would be able to sleep well tonight.

"They wanted to what?" he asked.

"Nothing. Let's find Jonnie."

"You start to talk and then you stop. You're making about as much sense as Mother."

"I'll check below deck and you check topside and on the ice. Okay?" I said, quickly changing the subject.

"Okay," agreed Michael and then went running off.

I started my search but with no enthusiasm. I knew we were on a wild-goose chase. They didn't want to talk to Jonnie. They just wanted to send us away so they could discuss what was happening, things they didn't want us to hear. Part of me longed to be in the galley, to be part of what they were saying, while the bigger part of me wished I could be like Michael and have no idea of what was ahead. Here I was, caught in the middle; too young to be included in their conversation, but old enough to worry about what it could be about.

9

I raised my hand to knock on the closed door. Beautiful music spilled out from under it. I hesitated for an instant and then knocked, quietly, and stepped back to wait for an answer. There was no reply. The music continued to flow. It had taken all my nerve to come here in the first place and now I had to fight the urge to flee. But I had to know the answer. I'd tried talking to Jonnie but he didn't seem to know anything more than I did. I thumped the palm of my hand against the door with such force the sound echoed down the corridor.

"COME!" came the response.

I opened the door and was hit by a wave of heat. Stepping into the room I was engulfed in both the warmth of the air and the sound of the music. Captain Bartlett was seated in a chair, sitting beside an enormous gramophone. His eyes were closed. On his lap sat Figaro, curled up in a sleeping ball.

"Captain Bartlett…"

He brought one finger to his lips and raised the other hand to silence me. I stopped. He lowered his hands, and his eyes remained closed. There was a look of total peace on his face as the music, the only sound in the room, swirled about.

I looked around. Over in the corner there was a small pot-bellied stove, the fire gleaming through the partially open grate. That explained why the room was so warm. Most of the cabins, including the one I shared with Mother and Michael, only had heat coming up through the vents from the boiler room. Over by the Captain, on a sturdy wooden table, sat his gramophone. Protruding from it was a big, black horn, which magnified the sound. Beside the player was a shelf containing hundreds and hundreds of records. The music came to an end. I looked over and Captain Bartlett opened his eyes.

"Mozart. Beautiful music ... so hauntin', an' majestic an' lonely. It reminds me of—"

"Up here," I interrupted.

A flash of white formed into a smile and shone through his beard. I was thrown by the smile. I didn't think he knew how to smile.

"Exactly. Ya surprised me, girl. Didn't think ya'd figure that. This is one of my very favourite pieces of music."

"I know."

"Ya do? How would ya be knowin' that?" he asked. A puzzled look crossed his face.

"Well ... it's just ... I mean ... I know that you play it every night."

"And how would ya know that? Are you listenin' at my door?"

"No! I mean, no sir, Captain! It's just at night, my bed is right by the wall and I can hear the music coming from your cabin."

"I'm real sorry, lassie. I didn't mean ta bother ya with my music."

"It's no bother, honestly! I love hearing the music!"

"Ya do? Interestin'. Music is a wondrous thing. No matter where I go I always bring my music with me. I have over two hundred recordin's right here with me. I don't figure ya ever saw a gramophone like this one," said Captain Bartlett, pointing at the machine on the table beside him.

"I've seen gramophones before, but nothing like yours."

"This here is the fanciest they make. Got it down in New York. It'll play for almost an hour each time I give it a wind. But … before I go on any more … ya didn't come in here to ask me about my music, did ya?"

"No, sir."

"Then what can I do for ya, missy?"

"Well…it's just I want to know about some things."

"Things? What sort of things do ya want ta know?"

"I was just … I don't know … I don't know how to ask it," I answered.

"Just spit it out. Ask away."

"Are we going to sink?" I blurted out.

"Not tonight," he chuckled and then stopped. I think he could see how worried I was. "What makes ya think we might be goin' under?"

"It's just that the ice is getting thicker and thicker. And I remember you saying the ship wasn't very strong. And you're having them bring all the supplies up on the deck and onto the ice. And…" I felt my lower lip start to quiver and I knew I was close to tears.

"But don't ya go worryin'. Things are all being taken care of," he said reassuringly.

"Then we're not going to sink?"

"I didn't say that."

I couldn't stop the tears any more and they ran down my cheeks.

"Now, now, Helen." Captain Bartlett took Figaro in his hands, stood up and gently placed the cat on the chair. He came over to my side and took a handkerchief from his pocket and handed it to me.

"Thank you," I said, taking it from him and dabbing away the tears while I fought hard to stop more from coming.

"We'll stay afloat…at least for a while."

"Long enough for Mr. Stefansson to return?" I asked hopefully. Somehow being on the ice with him seemed so much safer. I just knew he'd never let anything bad happen to any of us.

The Captain walked to the far side of the cabin and sat down on a chair framed by two large bookshelves.

"He's due back in a few days. Will we last that long?" I asked.

"Helen, there's no tellin' how long things will stay together. The ship may stand up ta the ice for hours, or days, or weeks or even months. Maybe we can even stay frozen in till spring. Who knows?"

"Spring? You mean we might be frozen in all winter?" I exclaimed.

"We're not goin' any other place till the ice leaves. Could be next May or even later, 'pending on the weather."

"But Mr. Stefansson will come back and get us and help us get to Herschel Island even if the ship is frozen in. Right?"

He opened his mouth to speak, and then closed it again without saying anything. He took a hand and started rubbing it against his thick beard, but he still didn't speak. As he sat there Figaro crossed the floor and jumped back onto his lap and snuggled in again. His silence made me feel more uncertain. My stomach started churning and I was afraid of what he was going to say when he finally spoke.

"Helen," he said quietly, looking me squarely in the face. "The plate of ice that has us has been driftin' since that first day we got grabbed. Thirty, sometimes forty or more miles every day. It just came inta shore fer a few days…when Mr. Stefansson got off…an' now we're drifting away again. There's water, open water, 'tween us and the shore."

"That's a lie! Mr. Stefansson wouldn't just leave us here! He's coming back to get us!" I practically shouted. "He's going to save us!"

"Nobody's goin' ta save us, save those that is with us."

"But … but … " I stammered, feeling confused and scared and, most of all, alone. I stood up and ran out the door, along the short strip of corridor, flung open the door of my cabin and threw myself onto my bed sobbing.

"Helen, what's wrong?"

I turned and saw Mother, sitting on the edge of her bunk. I hadn't noticed her as I ran into the cabin. Quickly she crossed the distance between our two bunks and placed both her arms around me. I tried to speak but instead I felt my whole body convulse with the power of the sobs. I threw my arms around her and buried my face into her chest. She started stroking my head with one hand, still holding me tight with the other arm, and made soft cooing sounds that I didn't understand but somehow were calming and soothing. She hadn't held me like this for so long. I tightened my grip. I didn't want to let her go.

As the tears started to subside, I pulled away and looked up into Mother's eyes.

"Feeling better?" she asked.

I nodded. Her holding me had made things better.

"Now tell me...what happened?"

I felt another swell of tears just below the surface, and bit my lip to keep them in check. "It's Mr. Stefansson..." I started to say and my voice broke.

"We'll do just fine without him, dear."

I pulled slightly back. "Without him? How did you know—"

"He wasn't coming back?" she interrupted, reading my mind and completing my sentence. I nodded. "I thought as much from the day he left. Why would he take so many supplies with him?"

"I didn't even know you'd seen everything," I said.

"I was taking a break and saw the goings-on from up there by the rail."

"But what will happen to us? What will we do if the ship sinks? I'm so afraid that we'll—"

Mother brought a hand up to my face and pushed a finger against my lips to silence me. "Captain Bartlett will take care of things," she said quietly.

"Captain Bartlett! I don't want him to take care of things! He hardly talks to us and he's so mean!"

"Helen, don't mistake hard for mean. A man has to be hard to survive in this land, and he's survived time and time again."

"But he didn't even want us to come along on the trip, and—"

Once again my mother interrupted me. "And I should have listened to him. This is no place for children, and if I had listened my children would be safe!"

"But you couldn't have just left us!" I objected.

"I could have, and I should have. I was so desperate to get the money to secure the future for you and your brother that I forgot about the present! I should never have allowed my children to be placed in such danger!

I should have found somebody to take care of you."

"No, you shouldn't have. We have to be with you. You can't ever leave us. Ever!"

As she started to answer, there was a knock on the door. Before either of us could rise, it opened slowly, and Captain Bartlett peered into the room.

"Excuse me, ladies," he said apologetically. "I was just wantin' ta make sure Helen was okay." He paused. "An' now that I see she's with her mama, I knows ya won't be needin' me, so I'll just be goin'." He started to close the door.

"Wait!" Mother called out, and he stopped. "Please, Captain, could you step in for a minute."

"Yes, ma'am," he answered and came into the room. He took his hat off and held it in front of him. She motioned for him to take a seat at the table and he followed her directions. Mother released me and as she stood up she straightened her dress.

"Captain, if I am to understand correctly, it appears Mr. Stefansson will not be rejoining our expedition. Is that right, sir?"

"Yes, ma'am."

"If it was possible to leave the ship and make for land at that time, why didn't the entire party abandon ship, Captain?" Mother asked.

"Mr. Stefansson wouldn't have known for certain he would make land. An' even then it wouldn't have been possible for all of us ta travel. Not enough dogs or sleds ta make such a trip."

"I see. Could I beg to ask one more question, Captain?"

"I'll answer all the questions ya have, ma'am."

"Thank you, Captain. Am I to understand from the preparations we are making, you believe we may have to leave the ship…that it may not survive the ice. Is that also correct?"

He nodded.

"Is there anything more I should know at this time, Captain?"

He thought for a few seconds before answering. "No, ma'am, I think that's pretty well the whole kettle of fish."

"Thank you, Captain," Mother replied.

He rose to his feet, and crossed to the still-open door. He started to pull the door closed and then paused. He turned back to face us.

"There is one more thing ya should know. Nothin' bad will be happenin' ta your children. I'll be gettin' 'em, an' everybody else off this ship, alive an' well. Ya have my word on that, ma'am."

10

I tried my best to fall asleep but I couldn't shut off the sounds of the ice. Popping, groaning, banging, grinding and smashing. Sometimes it sounded like voices calling out, or a baby crying or animals growling. We were frozen solid, but there was nothing solid about the water underneath the ice. The currents continued to flow and swirl and move and the ice was fractured into blocks that rubbed and crashed against each other. The noises could be separated by a few seconds, or a few minutes or even half an hour. They had been almost constant for the past three weeks, and tonight, they were louder and more frequent. They seemed to come just close enough together to stop me from dropping off to sleep. I closed my eyes tighter and tried to snuggle down lower inside my sleeping sack, as if somehow it could block out the sounds...and the danger those sounds meant.

There was a deep groan and I felt the whole ship shudder. I opened my eyes, but I couldn't see anything except the darkness of the cabin. I sat up. Something was wrong.

"Mother!" I whispered in alarm.

"Go to sleep, Helen, it's the middle of the night," her voice came back softly through the darkness.

"But something's wrong!"

"Nothing's wrong...it's just the ice...everything is

all right…"

"I think she's right, Mother," Michael chimed in.

"Isn't anybody asleep?" she asked and sighed deeply. "All right, let's get up and talk for a while. I'll light the lamp."

I heard her move her bed clothing. Then there was a crash, as if she had bumped into something.

"Oh, my goodness!" Mother called out.

"Mother!" I said in panic. I quickly pulled my legs out of the sack, scrambled out of my bunk and fell to the floor.

"It's all right, Helen."

I felt a hand at my side, helping me. I was unsteady on my feet and had to hold on to the side of my bunk.

"Stand still and I'll light the lamp," she said.

I watched the dim grey outline of her body move away and then heard the sound of a match being struck. I saw a small patch of light illuminate her hand and arm and then move on to the lamp. The glow grew quickly until the entire room was bathed in a soft yellow light.

What the light revealed was frightening! The floor was tilted and the room was on a terrible angle. During the night the ice had shifted, causing one side of the ship to rise up.

"Mother, what does this mean?" Michael asked.

"I don't know, but I want you both to put on your parkas, quickly. We must get onto the deck."

Michael tried to leap from his bunk but his feet were still tangled in his sleeping sack and he crashed to the floor. Mother lurched over and helped him up. Quickly we pulled on our parkas, mukluks and gloves. It was reassuring to put them on. They were soft and warm and were like a second skin. Michael and I were warned, over and over again, not to go out, especially onto the ice, without being covered.

It was difficult to move around the cabin. We stumbled and bumped into things, and finally got through the door into the corridor. I placed one hand against the wall to support me as we made our way towards the deck. Mother led the way carrying the lamp. Coming up to the hatch she passed the lamp back to me and put both hands against the door. At first it didn't budge. She put her shoulder against it and it popped open. I pulled up my hood to shield myself from the wave of cold air rushing in through the doorway.

The deck, of course, was on the same angle as the rest of the ship, but somehow it seemed even more shocking. I heard voices and turned. Standing against the railing, on the side of the ship aimed downward towards the ice, were most of the members of the expedition.

The air was cold and still. There was no wind to blow away the cloud of steam that came each time I exhaled. On unsteady feet we joined the party of men.

"Good evening, gentlemen," Mother began.

They all mumbled back greetings to us.

"Could someone please tell me what is happening here?" she asked.

"It's what's happening out there," Mr. Hadley said, pointing out onto the dim ice.

"Out where?"

His voice was drowned out by a surge of sound, followed almost immediately by a rush of air.

"What is that?" asked Mother as the din faded.

"Ice…crashing down. Two big pans are coming together, rafting up and then crashing down," Mr. Hadley explained.

"Where is Captain Bartlett?"

"He's on the ice, ma'am," Jonnie answered. "Went out ta try ta see what was what."

Mother asked, "Are we in any danger?"

"We're frozen in the ice, in the Arctic, coming into winter with no escape, Mrs. Kiruk. How can we not be in danger?" replied Dr. Mackay.

"I meant tonight. Are we in danger tonight?"

"It all depends on which direction the rift moves. It's like a meat grinder, eating up ice...and anything else that's on the ice. It's still far away...but it's coming closer all the time."

"Shouldn't we be doing something?" Mother asked.

"We is, ma'am. We's waitin' for the Cap'n ta come back an' give us orders," replied Mr. Anderson. "Meanways, I t'ink we should all go back ta bed an' try an' get some sleep."

Nobody answered, but a few members of the crew started to wander away from the railing. Just then the sound of crashing ice, like distant thunder, rumbled across the ice. Everybody stopped and turned towards the horizon. The few people who had started away turned back and stood against the railings, staring out onto the dark ice, trying to imagine what we couldn't see.

We all remained on deck, watching and waiting. It was almost four in the morning when we saw the outline of a dog sled moving across the ice towards us.

It was Mr. Stefansson coming back to get us! He'd found a way off the ice and to safety. He'd come onto the ship and we'd all follow him across the ice and everything would be fine...the hero returning to save the heroine at the darkest hour...

"Cap'n's coming in!" chimed in a voice.

I felt myself deflate. Of course it was Captain Bartlett. I put my fantasy away.

There was no place for it up here. I had to be grateful Captain Bartlett would soon tell us what was going to happen next.

People moved aft and down the stairs, onto the ice. There were now eight different ice buildings scattered around a central parade ground. In the centre a flagpole had been driven into the ice and a Union Jack hung down limply from the top. This was one of the few times it wasn't being blown about wildly by the winds.

The huskies were in teams, chained to stakes pounded into the ice. They got up and started pacing and snarling and barking at each other. They'd probably caught the scent of the returning dogs.

I walked over to a team of dogs and scratched Daisy behind the ear. She started sniffing the pockets of my parka until she found the scrap of food. I pulled out the treat and gave it to her.

Of course Daisy wasn't really her name. It was something in Inuit that meant flower but I couldn't pronounce the word, and since a daisy is my favourite flower, Michael and I called her Daisy. Kataktovick said she was a very smart dog. He always used her as his lead animal. He said of all the dogs she had the best sense when thin ice or a fresh lead was up ahead and she'd stop. He bragged how he'd never gone into the water with her at the head of his team.

Michael said something to Daisy. I couldn't understand what he said. I looked at him quizzically.

"I was telling her that she's a pretty dog," he said.

"It didn't sound like that to me."

"That's because you only understand English. Kataktovick is teaching me to speak some of his language."

"He is? He's teaching you Eskimo?"

"Inuktituk is what it's called. He's teaching me some words while I'm helping him to speak more English."

"His English is getting better," I admitted.

"But not as fast as I'm learning his language."

"Since when have you ever been interested in learning anything?"

"When it means something. This isn't like all that useless stuff you learn in school or in your romance novels."

"Leave my stories alone! Besides, what makes you think this is any more useful?"

"The dogs understand Inuktituk better than English. If you want the dogs to listen, you have to know their language."

"Don't be silly, Michael! I'm sure the dogs understand English..."

Michael barked out a guttural sound and Daisy instantly sat. Michael looked up at me with a huge smile on his face. "Guess what I just said to Daisy."

Rather than answer I quickly turned around. He was annoying enough when he was wrong.

Captain Bartlett was riding on the back of the sled, pushing along with one foot. He was accompanied by one of the Inuit hunters, who was running beside him. They pulled to a stop in the circle of ice buildings. Kataktovick moved to the front of the team of dogs and took hold of the lines. He led the dogs away and Michael followed. People quickly surrounded the Captain and began questioning him.

"Too tired ta talk right now...'sides, I have ta think before answerin'. I'll answer questions...in the morning ...eight hundred hours in the galley. Everybody go ta sleep," Captain Bartlett said.

He brushed aside people and started walking back to the ship. I tried to read the look on his face, to figure out how bad the situation was, but between the darkness and his heavy beard I couldn't see his expression clearly. He walked right up to and then by me.

"Captain Bartlett?" I called out.

He stopped and turned around to face me. "Yes, Helen?"

"Please tell me…tell us…what's going to happen."

He paused and removed his heavy gloves. "Fer now, nothin' will happen. First light, though, we need ta prepare."

"Prepare for what?"

"Ta abandon ship."

11

We all went back to our cabin and pretended to sleep. It felt strange lying in my bunk on such an awkward angle. I knew neither Mother nor Michael had fallen asleep, and I thought they knew I was still awake as well. I was far too afraid to even think that sleep was possible. After each crash I would start to count, slowly and carefully, hoping to reach a higher number each time. Instead the sounds came sooner and became louder and closer. The ship quivered and trembled repeatedly, and I felt, or imagined I felt, the ship tilting even farther over on its side. Towards the morning the noise started to fade away, and the crashes were farther and farther apart. Finally I counted and kept counting but no next crash came.

At last the ship's bells rang out, signalling eight o'clock. Wordlessly we all rose from our beds. I was relieved to see the ship had levelled out slightly. We hadn't undressed when we went to bed and my clothes felt moist and uncomfortable. We headed for the galley.

By the time we arrived, almost everyone was there. Nobody greeted us or even acknowledged we'd entered the room. There wasn't any conversation. People were just sitting, staring into their coffee cups. It was as though all their words had been used up, and judging by the piles of plates and jumble of mugs I suspected many of the men had been here for the whole night. As always the stove was glowing with heat and the room was hot and filled with the aroma of cooking and baking. Scanning the faces of the men, I realized the only one missing was Captain Bartlett. Almost as if thinking his name made him appear, the door opened again and he walked into the room.

He strode through the crowd. Men moved aside to let him pass. He walked over to the stove, and poured himself a mug of thick, black coffee. He took a small sip and then looked around the room, as though he hadn't noticed that we had all gathered there.

Finally he spoke. "Quiet as a funeral in here. Somebody die an' not tell the Cap'n?" he chuckled.

"I don't appreciate your gallows humour, Captain Bartlett," objected Dr. Mackay.

"I don't see any gallows," Captain Bartlett said, taking another long sip from his mug. "Nobody has died…an' nobody has ta die."

The room bubbled with noise as conversations and questions erupted from every part of the room.

"Quiet," he said and the room fell back into silence. He took another long pull from his coffee, tipping it up high. "I need ta tell ya what I know, an' thinks I know, an' what I have planned." He turned around and refilled his mug. "First thing. As ya all pretty well figured out, we're safe for now. The ice floes have stopped grinding each other down."

I let out a deep sigh and I could see smiles emerge from across the room, even though I didn't think it was really news to anybody except for maybe me and Michael.

"But…that doesn't mean we're safe for more than now. Sooner, more likely than later, this ship'll be goin' down. An' that means we have ta take ta the ice and sled our way ta safety."

"That is totally ridiculous!" objected Dr. Murray. "Are you suggesting we take all our scientific equipment by sled to Herschel Island?" He was an oceanographer and his equipment filled a large section in the hold of the ship.

"No, sir, I'm not. First off, we can't take any scientific equipment…"

"I will not just abandon my equipment! You have no authority to order me to abandon my equipment."

"I have total authority, sir. I am both the Cap'n of this ship an' the leader of this expedition…"

"Temporary leader…only in Mr. Stefansson's absence," interrupted Dr. Mackay.

The Captain took another sip from his coffee. I'd heard the scientists grumbling before this. They were prepared to let Captain Bartlett be the temporary leader of the expedition, but as it became more obvious that Mr. Stefansson was not able to return, they were less pleased to follow his leadership.

"Is there any man here fool enough ta believe Mr. Stefansson will be returning?" Captain Bartlett asked.

There was no answer and many turned their eyes to the floor.

"Good! At least we all know the truth. An' as long as I'm leadin' this party my orders will be followed. Understand?"

There was a heavy, explosive silence as everybody waited for a reply.

"I am certain Mr. Stefansson will not support your plan and you will suffer the consequences when we finally arrive at Herschel Island, Captain," Dr. Murray threatened.

"Herschel Island is not our destination," Captain Bartlett answered.

"What do you mean? Mr. Stefansson will be waiting for us there and expect us to continue our expedition," thundered Mr. Beauchat.

"Our goal, sir, is stayin' alive. Nothin' more, an' nothin' less. We want ta live. We can't reach Herschel. Each day we sit here in the ice, the ice keeps movin'. Twenty ta forty miles west, each day, farther away from Herschel. Is that not so, Dr. Murray?"

Dr. Murray looked uncomfortable, as if he didn't want to confirm what had just been asked.

"Is it not true, Dr. Murray?" the Captain repeated.

"I'm afraid so. My readings indicate movement in that amount, daily, depending on the ocean currents."

"Sledding tawards the east, even if ya could travel forty miles in a day, which no man here can, would just keep us in the same place. We have ta head ta the west."

"To the west! There's nothing to the west but open ocean."

"Siberia," Captain Bartlett said quietly. "We have ta cross the ice…find land…an' the only land we're going ta find is tawards Siberia."

"And do you suggest we leave right away?" asked Dr. Mackay.

"No gain. Ship's movin' where we want ta go. We have ta stay with her as long as she stays with us. There's always a chance, somehow, she'll stay afloat."

"As you are aware, Captain Bartlett, Dr. Mackay and I travelled by sled halfway across the Antarctic with Sir Ernest Shackleton. We covered much greater distances than our present position is from the shore," said Dr. Murray.

"Yep. Quite an accomplishment it was, sir, truly. I

am a great admirer of Sir Ernest, an' appreciate your expertise with dog an' sled. Your daring an' determination was truly inspirational."

"Very kind of you, Captain," Dr. Murray replied.

"An' I know when the time is right we're goin' ta be countin' on the two of ya very heavily for that expertise. But the thing here is that ya don't have any land under your feet. Between us an' land is plenty of open water an' shiftin' ice pans. Experienced men such as the two of ya might make it, but ya might not. 'Sides, I have to think of the lives of all the party. Do ya really want ta take young Michael or Helen 'cross the shiftin' ice?"

I felt all the eyes in the galley swing around and focus on Michael and me.

"Of course not, good man, but as you yourself stated, across the ice is our only escape."

"That's God's truth, sir. But, because I have ta travel the ice doesn't mean I can't travel it smartly. Firstly, as we sits here talkin', we're driftin' in the right direction. I'd rather move sittin' here drinking my coffee than on the back of a sled. Second, each day the ice gets thicker and safer ta travel on. Thirdly, this trip will take upwards of five weeks on the open ice and we have ta wait till the temperature rises an' the sun returns. Come late November we won't be seeing a sunrise till some time in February."

"February! Are you proposing that we don't take to the ice for three months!" shouted Mr. Beauchat.

The Captain rose from his seat and walked over to Mr. Beauchat. He placed a hand on his shoulder. "Yes, over three months, if the ship'll hold us. If she sinks we're goin' ta have ta take ta the ice sooner, but I can't see travellin' till mid-February."

"You cannot expect us to simply wait here for three

months doing nothing!"

"Nobody'll be just waitin'. We have ta work, and work hard if we're ta live ta see the shore."

"But you yourself have said this ship may not last more than a few days," said Dr. Mackay.

"That's right, Doctor, an' that's why our first job is ta move all supplies, 'specially food an' fuel, off the ship."

"That is preposterous!" Dr. Murray objected. "There must be tons of fuel alone."

"Twelve tons of coal, nearly forty cases of gasoline an' five barrels of alcohol. Wish we had us some more … not ta mention more time. As it is, each man, an' woman an' child, will be workin' harder than they ever have in their lives. If there are no more questions, it's best we put our noses ta the wheel an' begin."

12

Dear Diary,

I know it's been over a week since my last entry but I just haven't been able to do any writing. Partly it's because I've been so busy doing other things. As well, I guess because Mother has been even busier, she hasn't had time to remind me to write. The main reason though is that at the end of the day I'm just too tired to write. Working out in the cold drains away all my strength and makes my body ache all over. I've worked harder than I ever have in my life. Michael and I have to do the same work as the men. It's hard and the cold seems to draw the life right out of you and you get so tired so fast. I guess it doesn't help that we're bundled up in so many layers of clothing. Mother made me a pair of trousers like the men and I wear them whenever I go outside. As well, I keep tripping over my oversized mukluks which are now filled with layer upon layer of socks. Even with all of that, it still doesn't work. Whenever we're outside my feet get all tingly and numb and then when they start to thaw out it makes me cry in pain. A couple of times I've picked up my pen to start to write and my hands have been aching too much. I've just stopped and crawled into my sleeping sack.

The days have gotten shorter and shorter and last week the sun set and hasn't risen again. This night will last for almost three months. It doesn't just stay dark all the time, though. Each day there's a midday, high moon time. It isn't bright out, like it would be during a normal day, but there's enough light to see by. During this time everybody is outside, working hard. We helped move all the gear off the ship and into the ice camp. We've helped Mother stitch new clothing. Probably hardest of all, we've helped to build a wall of ice and snow around the ship. The sides and deck are all covered with a thick layer of snow. This is supposed to keep it warmer on board. I think it has helped but it's still cool inside. We have to wear our parkas all the time except for when we go to bed, but it's a lot better than outside.

The temperature keeps dropping. Yesterday it was more than forty degrees below zero. I think back to when Michael and I were standing inside that cooler in the restaurant and how that had seemed so cold. It was practically like a summer day. There's always blowing snow and the sound of the wind whistling around the ship is as constant as the sounds of the ice creaking and moaning under our feet. It's okay that we only have a couple of hours of moonlight to work by each day because it's almost more than I can bear to stay out any more than an hour at a time. After just a few minutes you can feel *your whole body start to ache. Dr. Mackay said at these temperatures exposed skin will freeze within minutes. When we're outside the only parts of us not covered by fur are our eyes. Even then we smear seal fat all over our faces for protection. I didn't want to do it at first, smear fat on my face, but without it your skin just freezes up. As it is, when the wind is blowing, which is almost all the time, bits of ice are thrown up in your face and it feels just like needles and pins.*

The warmest place on the ship is the galley and I spend a great deal of my free time there. I try and sit close to the stove. The heat flows out and into my body. It feels so good just to be warm. Cookie has been working hard fixing meals. We have enough food on board to last us for the entire length of the expedition. There are giant bags and barrels and crates and a mountain of canned food of all different kinds, so we can choose almost anything we like and eat as much of it as we want. One of my favourite things, though, doesn't come from our stocks. It's polar bear steak. Other than the fish caught through the ice it's the only fresh meat we have. The men have shot five bears. They keep wandering into camp, attracted by the light. I felt sorry after I saw the first one lying there, its red blood staining the snow and ice, but when I saw it up close, those teeth and claws, I was just glad they shot it. It was a male and stretched out was almost ten feet long. Jonnie said it probably weighed more than a thousand pounds. Cookie butchered it for the meat, right there on the ice.

Captain Bartlett has ordered us all to try

and gain more weight. He said it's like an extra layer of clothes to keep us warm as well as extra fuel to keep us moving. When we set off across the ice all the food and fuel we'll need has to be on our backs or on the sleds.

One of the other things that's always happening in the galley is chess. There's at least one pair of men playing and a few other boards, games in progress, sitting off to the side waiting for the players to return and finish. I've learned the game pretty well and I've played with a lot of different people. I even played the Captain once. We used his chessboard. The pieces were beautiful hand-carved ivory and felt so nice in my hand. The Captain beat me badly. When I play some of the men they go easy on me, but the Captain played to win.

I'm going to stop writing now. Mr. Hadley promised he'd have something special for us to do today.

I put aside my fountain pen and diary. I replaced the lid on the bottle of ink although the ink was now so thick from the cold I doubted it would spill out even if I tipped the bottle. I gathered up my outdoor clothing. Wearing trousers certainly felt strange but it was so much warmer and less cumbersome than a skirt.

The sky was clear and there was hardly any wind. The moon was high and bright and the ice reflected the light. I took a deep breath of the clean, cold air. I heard voices coming from the other side of the ship and wandered around the deck. At first I didn't see anybody. Then, looking up, I saw my brother along with Mr. Hadley and Jonnie standing on the top of the aft cabins.

"Helen! Come on up! Climb up the ladder," Michael called out.

I didn't want to climb anywhere but I did as he asked and soon was standing beside the three of them.

"Want to try?" Mr. Hadley asked.

"Try what?" I asked nervously, peering down at the deck below and the ice even farther down.

"Skiing," Michael replied.

"Skiing! What do you mean skiing?"

"What do you think these are?" Michael asked, gesturing to a pair of wooden slats attached to his feet. "Watch!" He waddled over to the side of the cabin and then dropped off the edge.

"YAHHHHOOOOO!" he screamed at the top of his lungs.

I watched him reappear on the ice below, slide across the ice and then skid to a stop. Cautiously I moved over to the edge of the cabin. There was a glistening slope of snow forming a hill from the edge of the cabin right down to the surface of the ice.

"You going to try?" Mr. Hadley asked.

"I...don't know...I'm not sure...I once read a story about skiing in the Alps."

"It's important that we do more than read about it. Everybody has to get comfortable on skis. Once we start moving we won't just be walking, but snowshoeing and skiing as well."

"But we won't be going down hills like this...just sliding along the ice...right?" I asked, looking for an escape.

"Your brother said ya'd be too scared to try it," Jonnie laughed.

"Did he?" I replied indignantly. "What does he know? Is there another set of skis?"

"Right here," Mr. Hadley replied.

Jonnie brought them over and placed them by my feet. He used strips of rawhide to bind them to my mukluks.

"Let me explain how it's done," Mr. Hadley said. "It's not hard. Bend at the knees and if you think you're going to fall…just sit down on your behind."

I hobbled forward until the front ends of the skis were overhanging the edge of the slope. I really didn't want to do this. I turned and looked back at Jonnie. I started to lose my balance and Jonnie grabbed me by the arm.

"Helen, maybe ya shouldn't be doin' this…I wouldn't wanna see ya gettin' yerself all banged up."

"I won't," I answered and hoped I was telling the truth. I pushed off. There was a rush of air and I felt my stomach rise up into my throat as I whizzed down the hill. In just seconds the slope flattened out and I slid across the ice until I came to rest right beside my brother. There were cheers from behind me and I stuck my tongue out at Michael. I turned around to take a bow and my feet got all caught up and I fell to the ice. This time even my brother joined in the cheering.

13

"I still don't see why it is necessary for us to be part of this trip," Mother protested.

"Sorry, but it's Cap'n's orders, ma'am," Jonnie apologized. "Does ya want me ta take the matter up with 'im?"

"No," she answered immediately. "That won't be necessary. The children would be disappointed if they couldn't go, and I wouldn't dream of letting them go without me."

Mother was half right; Michael was excited. I would have been quite content to simply remain aboard ship rather than take a trip across the ice. The only thing which made the trip seem possible to me was that we were going out with the Captain, Kataktovick and Jonnie. They would keep us safe I was sure … almost sure.

Our destination was an igloo a full day's travel from the ship. It was stocked with food and fuel and we'd be taking along more supplies to cache in the igloo. I knew everybody else could have been more helpful than Mother and Michael and me, but the Captain wanted all of us to have some experience on the ice before we had to finally leave.

There was often a team of dogs and men on the ice, going to and from the shelter or scouting even farther away. I still remember that terrible sense of dread when Captain Bartlett led the first team away, the sled loaded down with supplies.

I couldn't help but think of Mr. Stefansson and how he waved goodbye...and never returned. There isn't a day that goes by that I don't wonder whether he's alive or dead, and if he is alive why he didn't come back to get us. There's still a lot of anger amongst the men about Mr. Stefansson leaving. More than a few unkind words were directed his way until the Captain put a stop to it. He said Mr. Stefansson was still the leader of the expedition and he wouldn't tolerate any disrespect or disobedience.

Michael came rushing into the cabin. "It's time to go. Everything is ready!"

"Thank you, Michael. Tell the Captain we're on our way," said Mother.

I slipped on my parka and pulled my huge gloves from the pockets.

"Everything will be all right. There is nothing to be afraid of," said Mother, but her voice quivered ever so slightly.

I turned to her and was shocked by the expression on her face; she looked scared. I'd been so concerned about the trip it had simply slipped my mind that Mother had hardly set foot on the ice. If this trip was worrisome for me, it must be genuinely terrifying for her.

"And if you feel afraid you don't be shy about telling me. Sometimes what you need is just to be offered a word of reassurance. Don't be embarrassed if you need me by your side...if you need a pat on the back...or even a hug...don't be embarrassed...sometimes we're all afraid," she said.

Mother crossed the cabin and placed an arm around

my shoulder. I buried my face into her chest and she squeezed me so tight I could feel her strength beneath all the thick layers of clothing.

It was a clear, cold day and the only wind was at our backs and helped to push us along. The ice was smooth and flat and trails had already been broken through the pressure ridges. There were three teams of seven animals. Daisy was the lead dog on the first team and was being driven by Kataktovick and Michael. Both took turns riding and pushing the sled and then moving along beside it. Mother followed in the second sled with Captain Bartlett. She'd tried her best, but it was soon obvious she couldn't keep up the pace and the Captain did most of the work. Jonnie was in charge of the third sled. I was trying not to slow us down but I realized Jonnie was making his shifts almost twice as long as mine to give me more time to rest.

Captain Bartlett raised a gloved hand and yelled for the teams to come to a stop. Almost as one the dogs flopped to the ice. I came over to the side of the sled which was away from the wind and squatted down to use it as a wind break. It was always a lot warmer out of the wind.

"Here, take this," Captain Bartlett offered, handing me a piece of hardtack.

"No thank you, I'm not hungry."

"I didn't ask if ya was hungry an' this wasn't a suggestion ... it was an order. Ya have ta keep eatin' out here. It's like throwin' another log on the fire. Now eat it."

I bit into the hardtack. It was like chewing on a frozen piece of shoe leather. Michael was helping Kataktovick give the dogs some food and water. They

exchanged a few words in Inuktituk as they worked.
He'd continued to spend more and more time with the
Inuit and was probably on the ice more than he was on
the ship. Mr. Hadley had told me that Kataktovick had
three daughters but his only son had died before he
turned two. I guess he and Michael sort of helped to fill
the gaps in each other.

Michael glanced my way. He smiled and his dark
brown eyes flashed playfully. I was taken aback by how
much he looked like Father. People were always saying
how they could tell he was Father's son, but I didn't
always see the resemblance. Now, when I do see it, I
don't know whether it's reassuring or disturbing.

"How ya feelin', Helen?" Jonnie asked as he
slumped down beside me.

"Okay, I guess. How much longer do we have to
travel?"

"Little less than two hours should do it. Best be
travellin' soon afore we runs outta light. Don't want ta
be crossin' in the darkness."

I stood up and brushed off the snow. A cramp
gripped one of my legs and I grimaced in pain, working
the leg up and down to relieve the straining muscles.

"A cramp?" asked Jonnie.

I nodded.

"Be sure ta get lots of water inta ya. Best t'ing fer
cramps is water. Ya better start on the sled an' I'll take
ta my skis."

Just minutes before we reached the igloo, the wind
picked up tremendously. As soon as the dogs were
securely staked outside the entrance, we took shelter
where it was snug. The six of us set up our sleeping
areas squeezed together in the igloo. I made my bed

atop two large wooden crates which contained packages and cans of food that had been brought earlier by other teams. As well as the food there were extra blankets and canisters of kerosene and alcohol. The smell of the kerosene filled the space and made it seem even smaller.

When the lantern was extinguished, the igloo was thrown into complete darkness. I held up my hand and couldn't even make out its outline. I was suddenly overwhelmed by a wave of fear. I knew there were six of us all crammed together inside the shelter, but I felt completely alone. I listened for the sound of breathing, because it had always been reassuring in the cabin to hear Michael and Mother beside me at night. I couldn't hear anything except the sound of the wind. I felt my stomach start to crowd up into my throat and a sense of panic began to overtake me. My lower lip started to quiver and I bit down on it hard to stop myself from calling out. I knew I wasn't alone…I knew it would be okay…or did I? We were alone on the ice, separated from safety by hundreds of miles of shifting ice and open sea.

I couldn't contain myself and a whimper escaped my lips. Had anybody heard it? What would they think of me for crying?

"It's all goin' ta be all right," Captain Bartlett said, his voice cutting through the lonely darkness. "It's all goin' ta be all right…just put your mind someplace else …think of a warm an' happy place…an' let yourself go visitin' there…it'll be fine in the end…just fine."

I didn't have to strain to think of a place. I closed my eyes and I was sitting on the bed in my old room, propped up on pillows, reading a book, with a cup of tea on the bedside table. I surrendered to the dream.

14

"...an' knew her not till she had brought forth her first-born son; an' he called his name Jesus." The Captain paused. "An' that is our Bible readin' from Matthew, Chapter 1, verses 18 ta 25. Could we all bow our heads in prayer fer the birth of the baby Jesus that took place on this day, in Bethlehem."

I lowered my head. There was silence save for the roar of the wind. I tried to pray, but my mind was caught by the distance and differences between the place of Christ's birth and the place where I stood.

"Amen," Captain Bartlett said loudly and echoes of "amen" came from every corner of the packed galley. Almost instantly people started filing out through the door. There was hardly a word spoken. Looking into the solemn faces of the men I could see a few close to tears.

I followed Michael and Mother. When we reached our cabin, we quickly prepared for bed. Even Michael didn't seem to have anything to say as he readied himself.

This was so different from any other Christmas I had ever experienced. The Captain had tried to fill us with the Christmas spirit. He'd organized the church service, carol singing, and even had Cookie prepare a special Christmas feast, but there was nothing that could drive away the feeling of loneliness or the sound of the wind outside the walls of the ship.

My thoughts went back to the last Christmas we'd spent together as a family. Father had been sick for months but he seemed to be much better. He was still very thin and stooped over but he was happier. He'd gone out with Michael and cut down the biggest tree that could fit in the room. It tired him out so much he had to lie down and sleep after returning home. Mother had trimmed it with tinsel and balls and cranberries and popcorn on a string and put a few candles on the tree. It looked beautiful. Under the tree were presents; but not many because the medicine and doctoring costs had been so great. The air was filled with the smell of the pine tree and the candles and the Christmas pudding simmering on the stove. We went to church Christmas Eve and I sang in the children's choir. That night when we were tucked into bed I knew, just knew, everything would be all right, that my prayers had been answered, and things would be back to the way they were, that Father would be okay. Three days later he died. Mother said that he wanted to have one more Christmas with us and we should be grateful his last wish was granted.

I was startled out of my thoughts by a knock on the door.

"Come!" Mother called out.

The door inched open and Captain Bartlett peeked in. "Sorry ta disturb ya, ma'am," he said quietly, "but I have somethin' for the children."

My ears perked up and Michael sat up on his bunk. He came into the room and closed the door behind him. Under one arm he carried two parcels. They were covered in cloth held together with pins. He handed the smaller of the two parcels to Michael and the other to me.

"This is very nice of you, Captain," said Mother.

He looked like he was going to blush, although it would be hard to tell since the only exposed parts of him, his cheeks, were weathered and red already.

"Ya goin' ta open 'em or just gawk?" he asked.

Neither of us needed any more prompting. Michael tore into the wrapping. Before I'd even taken the first pins out of my wrapping he was waving his present in the air.

"Thank you, thank you so much!" he screamed. He was holding a brass telescope, one that I'd seen before on the bridge of the ship. "It's wonderful!"

I removed the cloth from my present and there was a wooden box. I recognized it instantly. I undid the latch carefully, and opened the box to reveal the graceful figures of the carved chess pieces. Sixteen white and sixteen black men all sitting proudly in their spots. I looked up at Captain Bartlett.

"I hope ya like yer present as much as Michael likes his."

"I…I…don't know what to say…."

"These are such generous presents, Captain. Not necessary in the least," Mother said.

"My pleasure, Mrs. Kiruk. 'Sides, I thought these things were meant for your children. A telescope 'cause Michael is always tryin' ta see inta the future, always climbin' the riggin' ta see what's ahead. An' the chess set fer Helen 'cause she's always thinkin' things through. Besides, I've seen she was partial ta these pieces."

"But…but I can't take it," I said.

"I thought ya'd like 'em," he answered, sounding

confused.

"I do, I do!"

"Then, why?"

"It's just that…well, I mean…it's just I know how important these chess pieces are to you."

"They's just pieces…nice pieces, but nothin' more."

"But…we didn't get anything for you."

"Ya surely did. Watchin' ya both open your presents made me think about Christmas back home in Brigus with all my nieces and nephews. That memory was a nice present ta give me."

"Captain, may I ask you a question?" Mother asked.

"Sure thing, ma'am."

"I was wondering if you were still angry at me for bringing the children on the voyage."

"Angry at you? No ma'am, can't say I'm leastways angry at you, but I am angry. Even more than before."

"At who? Who are you angry at?"

"At myself. Never should have let your children come aboard. Whatever happens is all on my shoulders." He paused. "But enough…not tanight. A merry Christmas and good night ta ya all."

15

The storm had been raging hard for almost twenty-four hours. Strong winds and blowing snow had made it impossible to see any more than a few feet away even at midday, and now, as the high moon set, it was like a wall of white. Michael wanted to go out and help with the dogs, something we did every afternoon, but we weren't allowed. Nobody was allowed to leave the ship. It was too dangerous to travel even the few feet from the ship to the ice shelters.

I had no wish to go outside. It was so much better to lie on my bunk and read. Our cabin was feeling more and more like home. The Captain had lent me a book about gardening. He had a wonderful collection of books and he invited me to borrow one anytime I wished. I was so grateful since I'd long ago exhausted the supply of books we'd packed for the voyage. It struck me as strange to be reading a book on planting a garden when the nearest living blooming plant was over a thousand miles away.

Suddenly I felt the ship shudder. It was a long, low vibration that seemed to move from one end of the vessel to the other. There was a strange noise, different from anything I'd heard before. It sounded like an orchestra being tuned up. It surprised and scared me. Since the weather had gotten colder the ship seemed to have become just part of the ice pan and hadn't moved or shifted for weeks. I put down the book and hurried from the cabin.

Stepping into the corridor I almost bumped into Captain Bartlett, who was moving quickly in my direction.

"Where's your brother an' mother?"

"I saw Michael in the galley and I think Mother is working in the shop."

"Go an' get her, an' then get ta the galley," he ordered. Without even breaking stride he continued down the corridor, past our cabin.

"But Captain, what is—"

"No time for questions, Helen, just do as ya was told! Now!" he barked harshly. Without even turning around he raced around the bend and was gone. I stood there, stunned.

Suddenly the ship lurched violently. I lost my footing, stumbled and braced myself against the wall. I think I had the answer to my question. I raced along the corridor and started down the stairs. As I grabbed the railing, I heard footfalls against the metal and caught sight of Mother rapidly climbing up. Even in the dim light of the lamp I could see she was worried.

"Helen?"

"You have to come, right now, to the galley. I think something is happening to the ship, something bad," I answered.

"Where is your brother?"

"I think he's already in the galley. That's where I left him earlier today."

"You go to the galley. I'll go back to the cabin, just to make sure he hasn't gone back there looking for us."

"But, Mother, Captain Bartlett said we were to go

to the galley, immediately." I tried to impress upon her the urgent nature of things.

"Sorry, dear, a mother doesn't have to listen to anybody when her children are involved. Besides, I think you might be needing your mukluks," she said, pointing down at my feet.

I looked down. In my rush to leave the cabin, I hadn't even realized I was in my stockinged feet. Mother put her hands on my shoulders, spun me around, and gave me a small push. "Now go!" I took the first few steps up the stairs, and then stopped and watched her head back for our cabin.

Entering the galley I was relieved to see Michael. He was sitting at the table, a plate of cookies in front of him. All around him was almost everybody else in the expedition. I knew Kataktovick and the other two Inuit were already on the ice. They'd taken to living there, with the dogs, to protect them from a polar bear attack or in case the ice opened up. Also missing from the meeting were Captain Bartlett, his first mate and a couple of members of the crew.

Before I'd taken a seat, Mother entered, carrying my mukluks and an armful of clothing. Captain Bartlett entered right behind her and the noisy conversations drained away to silence. I pulled on my boots while everybody waited for him to speak.

"The ice that has been raftin' durin' this storm has hit us mid-ship. We've been twisted an' lifted an' turned an' holed. Twelve-foot hole, below the waterline. Only thing stoppin' us from sinkin' is that we're sittin' on the ice that holed us. Soon as the ice shifts back, the ship will go ta the bottom."

"Surely you can close the bulkheads or seal off the compartments or do something to keep the ship afloat!" declared Dr. Murray.

"Wish it was that easy. The hole goes inta both main holds. Besides, sir, the timbers all up an' down the ship have been twisted, some splintered an' a couple snapped right off in two. She's goin' down. Can't waste any time tryin' ta stop what can't be stopped. 'Stead we have ta use the time we have ta salvage what we can an' get it onta the ice."

Dr. Murray stood up and then cleared his throat as though he was going to speak.

"Something ya was wantin' to say?" Captain Bartlett asked.

He shook his head and sat back down.

Captain Bartlett pulled out his pocket watch. "It's 17:35. Ya all have till 18:00 hours ta gather tagether your belongin's an' assemble by the aft hatchway. It's time ta abandon ship."

"What sort of things should we be bringing?" asked Mother.

"Things ya'll be needin' for the ice. If ya can't eat it, wear it, or burn it...forget it."

People scrambled out of their seats and started pushing towards the door.

"One more thing!" the Captain called out and everybody froze. "If ya hear the ship's bells ringing, drop what you're doin' an' get ta the deck right away. The bells will be tellin' ya that she's going down...now."

Michael and Mother moved around the room, packing, while I just stood and stared. I knew we had to hurry but I felt myself slowing down. A few short weeks ago I'd hated this cabin but now it was like my home. It was safety and warmth and a place to hide from the ice and snow and freezing cold. I could just lie on my bunk and read a story and escape. Now it was being taken away. Something else being taken away.

"Come, Helen, it's almost time," Mother said quietly.

I broke out of my trance. Carefully I placed my chess set and a few pictures into the bag with my clothing. Next I rolled up my sleeping sack and tied it with twine. Michael was already waiting in the corridor and Mother was standing at the door. As I walked over she moved out. I grasped the handle, took one look back, and closed the door behind me.

By the time we reached the hatchway the corridor was crowded. The Captain stood by the hatch. Suddenly it opened and Jonnie came in, pushed by a wave of wind and snow. Somebody pulled the door shut behind him.

"That's some terrible storm."

"Jonathan...ya done your job?" asked the Captain.

"Yes, sir, Cap'n."

The Captain nodded approvingly. "Jonathan has strung out a guide rope from the ship right ta the ice shelters. Don't just keep an eye on the line...keep a hand on it. Mrs. Kiruk, Helen and Michael, leave your things here. Ya go in the first group. Jonathan...Mr. Hadley... I want the two of ya ta go with 'em ... make sure of things."

Jonnie led the way, pushing the hatch open. I lowered my head and braced myself against the rush of wind. Hitting the deck I stopped and looked around. My face stung from the driving snow and I had to fight to keep my eyes open. I couldn't see anything beyond the back of Jonnie's parka hood.

"Keep moving!" Michael yelled over the howl of the wind as he bumped into me from behind. Michael moved past me and as I started forward again my feet slipped. A pair of hands grabbed me roughly around one arm and pulled me up. I looked up and recognized Jonnie. He kept hold of my arm and we walked, side by side, along the deck. Despite the bitter cold I felt a surge of warmth underneath all my clothing—I was blushing. I was grateful for his support as we came to the stairs and started down on the ice. The bottom of the stairs, only fifteen feet below, was completely obscured by the snow. Michael, a few steps ahead, was a faint outline and Mr. Hadley, somewhere in front, was invisible.

Just as the Captain had said, there was a rope tied to the bottom railing. It led away in the direction of the shelters. Jonnie let go of my arm and took my hand, placing it on the rope. He faced me and bent down so the hoods of our parkas touched together.

"DON'T LET GO…DON'T LET GO!" he screamed so his voice could be heard over the raging wind. I nodded and we started to move.

I'd walked between the ship and shelters hundreds of times. It wasn't far—a straight line across smooth ice. But now it was all so different; the wind pushed against me so strongly I had to fight for each step forward. The snow, driven by the wind, swirled around me and I could see nothing beyond a few feet. I looked up but I could no longer make out even the grey shape of Michael ahead of me. I turned around. Jonnie was lost from sight as well. Except for the snow, all I could see was the rope, suspended in mid-air, stretching away from my hand. I stopped, frozen in place not by the cold but by fear. I knew that in one direction lay the ship, and in the other, the ice shelters, but I felt completely isolated. And without that thin strand of rope, my lifeline, I'd be wandering through the blizzard, lost

and desperate until I finally collapsed and died and a
polar bear found my carcass and… I got a grip on my
imagination and held the rope even tighter, with both
hands. I put my head down and shuffled on. Within a
half-dozen steps I made out the outline of the first
building. I dropped to my knees and then onto my belly
so I could crawl through the long, narrow entrance.
Going in was always harder than coming out because
the tunnels were built to rise up into the igloo. This
kept the warmer air inside from escaping. Instantly I
was protected from the wind and snow. I pushed
through the curtain blocking the room from the tunnel
entrance. There was an oil lamp glowing in the corner
and it lit every corner of the curved structure. It felt
warm, or at least warm compared to outside. I knew it
had to be below freezing though or the shelter would
have started melting.

Jonnie offered me a hand and helped me to my feet.
Michael was sitting on a cot. Another figure came
through the tunnel and again Jonnie offered his hand.

"Thank you, Jonathan," Mother said. As she pulled
down her hood, I could see she looked scared.

"Where's Mr. Hadley?" asked Michael. There was
concern in his voice.

"He's got back ta the ship already. I've gotta go too
an' help the next party ta their shelter. You're ta stay in
'ere till the storm blows off."

"Jonnie…"

He looked at me quizzically.

"Be careful…please."

"Be as careful as can be. Ya got me word on 'er."

He bent down and pushed back the curtain. A blast
of wind blew in through the opening. He turned
around. "Don't leave, for no reason…we'll see ya in

the morning."

I sat on one of the low wooden benches which served as a bed frame. It was made out of storage crates and wasn't comfortable, or meant to be. It was only designed to raise the sleeper a little bit off the ice. Once we started travelling these cots would be left behind and we'd have to sleep on skins, right on the ice.

There were two caribou skins underneath my sleeping bag and another piled on top. I pulled my legs up and then scrunched down even lower into my sack. I buried my head in the covers to try to escape the crying of the wind. The sound still penetrated. It whistled and roared and screamed. At times it sounded almost like an animal calling or a person screaming. I tried to block out the sound, but in the total darkness of the shelter there was nothing else to focus on.

I thought back to just last week, when I'd been out on that overnight sled trip and we'd slept in an igloo. That night started out scary but it became fun, like an adventure. This was so different. It wasn't just one night in the cold with my soft bunk in the cabin to go back to.

My feet felt hot and itchy in my mukluks but I didn't dare take them off. I remembered the stories about the ice opening up in the middle of the night, right underneath people as they slept. In one story the gap was between them and the entrance, and they had to jump across the open water to survive. That thought sent a chill right up my spine. I didn't know if I'd ever get to sleep.

I could hear voices…coming from outside the ice shelter. It was pitch black inside but I felt, or maybe just hoped, it was morning. I sat bolt upright in my bed.

"Mother?" I called out tentatively.

"Yes, dear, it's okay."

"I think it's morning. Can I...I mean can we get up?"

"I think so. Just stay there while I light the lamp." She struck a match and lit the lamp. I averted my eyes for a moment from the bright flame. Michael sat up, stretched and then rubbed his eyes. I heard voices coming through the walls again. I was anxious to see what was happening.

"I'm going to go and peek out," I said.

"Me too!" Michael announced.

"Wait!" ordered Mother. "We were told to stay inside. Let me go out first...I must make sure the storm has passed."

As she spoke, I realized the sound of the wind was gone and I was sure the storm had passed. Michael and I jostled together, trying to get out behind Mother. I was able to push him out of the way and he muttered something under his breath. I crawled forward. It was, of course, still dark—not the pitch black of night but the dim darkness of morning. There was just enough light to see by.

I was relieved the storm had gone. I looked around but there was nobody in sight. I didn't know where the voices had been coming from. The *Karluk* was still there, although it was clearly tilted. Along the side, well up from the ice, there was a long dark gash where it had been split open. I caught sight of movement and saw two men coming down the stairs, carrying something between them. Another figure crawled out of one of the igloos and came towards us. I couldn't make out who it was underneath the hood.

"Hello. Did you all sleep well?" It was Mr. Hadley.

"Could have been better," Mother answered. "And

yourself?"

"Sleep, ha! Didn't get any of that last night. The Captain had us up removing things from the ship. We've taken off anything that might be of value."

"Where is everybody now?" I asked.

"Mostly sleeping, just a few of us left working."

"Did they get my sewing machine off?"

"One of the very first things, ma'am."

The air was calm. It was still very cold. Our breath came out in billows of steam, but without the wind it didn't seem bad at all.

"It's good the storm has passed," I observed.

"Good and not so good," said Mr. Hadley. "The wind was the thing pushing against the ice, keeping the *Karluk* afloat. Now that it's died down it's just a matter of time before she settles back into the water...and then down to the bottom."

I turned back towards the ship. It looked so big and the hole so small I couldn't believe it was a fatal wound. I couldn't imagine the ship sinking. At that instant there was a groan and the ship shifted slightly. I gasped.

"She's been doing that for the past few hours. Ever since the wind died," Mr. Hadley observed.

"I'm hungry," Michael said. As always, his stomach was the only thing on his mind.

"Perhaps we should go for breakfast," Mother suggested.

"Sounds good," agreed Michael.

"I'm not hungry." Although I hadn't had anything since supper yesterday, I felt too nervous to eat.

"Helen, you really should eat," Mother said.

Michael started towards the ship. "I'll start eating while you two talk."

"Where do you think you're going?" Mr. Hadley

asked. Michael stopped in his tracks. "If you want breakfast it's being served in the big ice shelter at the end."

"Why can't we eat in the galley?" asked Michael.

"The ship's been abandoned. You know that."

"But you said it could be hours before the ship goes down. It won't take me that long to eat," Michael protested.

"Everything's been taken off the ship and onto the ice. Besides, it could go down sooner, and when it goes down it could go down fast," Mr. Hadley answered.

"Of course, Mr. Hadley," said Mother. "Michael, you must understand we're not allowed back on board. Everybody has left the ship."

"Almost everybody," Mr. Hadley replied. "The Captain is still aboard."

"Why is he still on board?" I asked anxiously.

"Just checking things ... maybe he's thinking about going down with the ship."

"He wouldn't really do that, would he?"

"Of course not!" Mr. Hadley replied. I think he realized just how worried I was. "I was just kidding ... I didn't mean for you to take me seriously, Helen. He's just making the rounds of the ship ... making sure we've taken off what we need ... making sure nobody is on board. Don't worry about Captain Bartlett."

"I'm not worried," Michael interrupted. "I'm hungry."

"Come on, then," chuckled Mr. Hadley. "Why don't we all go and get a little breakfast. Okay?"

"Thank you. As always we'd enjoy your company," said Mother. "Helen?"

"I don't want to eat now. I'm just going to go back to our shelter and write a little bit in my di—" As I tried to finish the sentence, I realized I'd left my diary behind. I wasn't sure why, but I didn't want to tell Mother I'd forgotten it in my rush to pack.

"All right, Helen, but please join us when you finish," Mother instructed.

I watched Michael run ahead and Mother and Mr. Hadley walk off behind him. I observed them until they dropped to the ground and disappeared into the tunnel.

I now stood alone on the ice. Everybody else was tucked inside a shelter, except for Captain Bartlett, who was still aboard the *Karluk*.

Without even thinking, I found myself moving towards the ship. I felt almost a magnetic pull, drawing me closer. I walked until it towered over me and all I could see were its dark sides, almost completely hidden by the snow and ice we'd packed for insulation. Right in the middle of the ship I could see the hole. It was a jagged, open wound stretching for at least a dozen feet. I looked inside but couldn't make out anything in the darkness.

Then I heard sounds coming out of the hole. At first it was too soft to make out what it was. Then, it became clearer. I smiled. It was Mozart. Captain Bartlett was listening to his gramophone. I could picture him in his favourite seat, sipping coffee from his mug, his eyes closed, lost in the music.

I thought about how much I enjoyed the music. How I'd lie in my bunk at night and listen or sit at the desk and write in my diary…my diary. I let out a long, deep sigh. I'd been recording my thoughts in that book for the past two years. Mother gave it to me just after Father got sick. She'd said that sometimes we can write about what we can't talk about. For the first year, every night I wrote about things that had happened to me that day. And, like Mother had said, I wrote about things I couldn't talk to anybody about. About how much I missed him and how sad I felt and how worried I was that something would happen to her. Things I couldn't burden Mother with.

She also showed me her old diary, the one she'd written when she was young, and we talked about how one day I would show my diary to my daughter. At least I would have if I hadn't left it on the ship. A thought started forming in my mind.

I turned around and looked over at the camp. There was no sign of anyone. If I went right now, quickly and quietly, I could go on board, retrieve my diary and get off the ship without anybody seeing me. It would only take a minute. Surely nothing could happen in a minute.

16

I moved quickly towards the rear of the ship. Within a few paces the faint strains of music emerging from the gash in the side of the ship faded away. I placed a hand on the railing and a foot on the bottom step and then stopped. I nervously looked back towards the camp. There was still nobody in sight. Nobody to see me if I went on board; nobody to think I was "chicken" if I didn't. There was just me. I took a deep breath and started up the stairs.

Within a few steps I realized the staircase was bent out of shape. The bottom was still frozen into the ice while the top was attached to the ship. The shifting of the ice had caused it to twist.

Once again I stopped, this time at the very top of the stairs. I thought about the trip across the deck, through the hatch, down the stairs, along the corridor and into our room. I wasn't sure why I was making this into such an adventure. I could stroll down, pick up my diary, and be back on the ice in less than three minutes. The ship was still anchored solidly in the ice and couldn't possibly sink that fast.

I started forward again. My footfalls were soft. The deck was still hidden below the ice and snow we'd packed on top to protect us from the worst of the winter weather, and it was horribly slanted towards the starboard side. The hatch door was closed. As I opened it, I was relieved to see there was light coming from below. Thank goodness the lamps were still burning. I started to close the hatch tightly behind me, the way I'd been taught to keep out the wind and cold, but thought better of it. I didn't want a closed door between me and the deck.

I placed a hand on the centre pole and started down the circular stairs. Before I'd reached even halfway down I was greeted by the sound of Captain Bartlett's music. It reminded me I wasn't alone on the ship. That was good…and bad. I didn't want the Captain to catch me aboard after he'd ordered everybody off. I had seen the way he reacted to anybody who disobeyed his orders.

At the bottom of the steps I was greeted by more light from the corridor. The music became louder. My mukluks didn't make much sound as I walked, and whatever noise they did make was masked by the music.

I eased myself along the wall. As I turned the corner I stopped. The door to Captain Bartlett's room was open. The glow from the lamps in his cabin spilled out into the hall, making it even brighter. I couldn't get to my cabin without passing right by his open door.

I had to think. I could just go back out to the ice and no one would be any wiser. It was foolish to even be here. It would be best if I simply left. But then I wouldn't have my diary, and all my thoughts and memories would be gone forever. I'd lost too much already. There was another way. I could go back up on deck, along the length of the ship, in through the forward hatch and double back to my cabin from the opposite direction. That way I wouldn't have to pass by the Captain's room. As soon as I thought this through, I knew I couldn't do it. I would have to pass right by the open gash in the main hold.

The only other option was to sneak by without being seen. Maybe he wasn't even in his cabin. And even if I was seen, what was the worst thing that could happen to me? I'd get my diary and then he'd escort me off the ship. Having an escort didn't sound bad at all. Of course, the thought that Mother would find out about it didn't bring me any comfort. It was no good. I had to leave, and leave now. I turned and started back out. I pressed myself flat against the wall and inched down the corridor.

"What in God's name!"

I froze in mid-step, with my eyes closed. If I kept my eyes shut tightly enough maybe he wouldn't see me.

"Helen, what are ya doin' on board?" he demanded.

Closing my eyes hadn't worked. I turned to face him. He was standing in the corridor by his cabin door.

"Nothing, sir... I mean I was just going to my cabin... to get my diary... I forgot it when I packed my things."

He looked at me long and hard. "Is ya by yourself?"

"Yes, sir."

"Ya sure Michael isn't climbin' up in the riggin'?"

"He's having breakfast. With Mother and Mr. Hadley. Mr. Hadley told us everybody had worked all night, taking important things off the ship. When are you taking off your gramophone?"

"I'm not," he said quietly.

"But you have to!"

"Can't work in the cold of the ice hut and can't take her on any sled. She'll go down with the ship."

"Is that why you're still here, to listen to your

music?" I asked.

"That an' ta read a little more. Never can get too much of the good book," he said, tapping the open Bible which he held in his hands. "Always strikes me as strange how much more sense it all makes up here. Down south there are always so many people, an' machines, an' inventions, an' buildings, an' things. Gets ta the point where ya can't look any way without seeing somethin' belongin' ta man. An' when all ya see is people an' their products ya start ta think we're just so important, just at the centre of everything. But ya come up here an' soon realize just how small an' insignificant we truly are. On that ice we're just one of God's creatures…an' our lives can be snatched away with the…" He paused. "Just brings ya closer ta the truth." He stopped. "It may sound funny but this place has become my home. Do ya miss your home, Helen?"

I nodded.

"What was it like?"

"Michael and I were born in Killington. It's a mining town in the interior, in the mountains."

"Is it a big place?" Captain Bartlett asked.

"Not very big, at least compared to Vancouver, but it's nice, really nice. The mountains are all around and there are trees and trails and we lived in a house that sits on a beautiful lake and…" I was struck by such a terrible sense of loss I couldn't go on.

"An' your father, was he a miner?"

I nodded.

"Ya must miss it something awful."

Again the words stuck in my throat and I could only nod.

"Well, when this is all over ya can return ta your home an' this'll be nothin' more than a memory."

"No, we can never go back," I blurted out. "The house ... the house isn't ours. It belongs to the mining company. After Father's death they let us stay on but then the mine expanded and they had to put another family there ... it isn't ours to go back to ... we can never return."

At that instant the music ended. Captain Bartlett disappeared into his cabin and I followed him. He removed the record from the gramophone and set it down gently. He put another record on the turntable and carefully placed the needle on it. Once again the room was filled with music.

"This one we just heard is one of my favourites," said Captain Bartlett.

I knew it well. It was one of my favourites as well. He held it delicately by the sides so as not to scratch the surface.

"Come on over here, Helen. I'll show ya something ya've probably never seen before."

He was now standing beside his black, pot-bellied stove, which was radiating warmth. He motioned for me to come closer.

"Goodbye, old friend," he said quietly, and tossed the record into the open mouth of the stove. In shock I watched as the disc collapsed into a black puddle and then burst into bright flames. The Captain turned to face me and could read the look of disbelief on my face.

"No room ta take 'em. No room for nothin' but food an' fuel."

"But ... " I stammered.

"Thought it best ta put 'em out of their misery. Better ta burn than ta sink ta the bottom of the ocean. Do ya know how deep the water is right below us?"

I shook my head.

"Neither does anybody else. Deepest part of the ocean. The Arctic's abyssal deep. They know for sure it's more than a mile an' a half down. So deep there's no warmth an' no light. So deep that once the ship starts sinkin', it'll keep droppin', farther and farther, for the better part of ten minutes before it reaches the bottom."

That thought became frozen in my mind...imagine being aboard the ship as it sank lower and lower and lower...helpless...helpless.

Captain Bartlett walked back across the room and took a seat in his favourite chair. Almost immediately Figaro jumped onto his lap.

"Sit," he said, motioning me to the other chair.

I hesitated before sitting. "Is it safe? Shouldn't we be getting off?"

"Ya should already be off, but don't worry, I'll know when she's goin' down. I've spent my whole life listenin' for the sounds of the ice. I'll know."

We sat without talking for a while. I tried to concentrate on the music but instead found myself trying to listen for any sounds coming from the ice.

"Is your family religious, Helen?"

"I guess so. We go to church."

"Church. I was just thinkin' about church. Back in Brigus, that's where I'm from, Brigus, Newfoundland, the church is the centre of everythin'. Weddin's, funerals, baptisms, an' celebrations. I remember, as just a wee lad, the minister tellin' us all about Heaven an' Hell. Heaven sure seemed like a fine place, but Hell... all full of fire an' brimstone, an' steam an' flame." He stopped and looked directly at me. "He was wrong about Hell, you know, dead wrong."

"You don't believe in it?" I asked hesitantly,

shocked by such blasphemy.

"Oh no, I sure as certain do," he answered. "It's just he was wrong about what's in Hell. It doesn't have any flames. It's freezin' cold. So cold yer body just aches. An' it's filled with drivin' snow so ya can't see your hand before your eyes, an' so lonely, there isn't another soul for ya ta see. It's…" He stopped abruptly. "I shouldn't be talkin' like this. Ya don't need ta be scared more than ya is already."

"I'm not scared…not that scared," I answered.

"You're not? I figured ya been scared almost every day since he left."

"Not really…at least not every day. I guess I missed him more in the beginning. It gets easier."

"Most things do. My old gramma used to say 'time heals all wounds,' and I think she was right."

"At first I was angry at him. Leaving us all behind. But I realized that it wasn't his fault. He didn't want to go away and leave us."

"It's good ya aren't blaming him."

"Well, I did at first. I think it was more than a year before I didn't feel mad at him," I answered.

Captain Bartlett looked confused. "Helen, is ya talkin' about your father?"

"Of course…who else would we be talking about…?" I let the sentence trail off as I realized he meant Mr. Stefansson. I felt so stupid.

"I'm sorry, Helen. That was my fault. I should have said things more clearly, 'stead of beatin' round the bushes. I know how hard it is ta miss your father. My old man died a few years back. I miss talkin' to him and tellin' him what's happenin' in my life. I can only imagine how hard it would be ta still be a child when your father passes over."

"That's all right…I'm fine," I answered.

"I know ya're all right, Helen, but it's all right ta miss him still."

I nodded in agreement. I felt numb and embarrassed. "I don't even want to talk about Mr. Stefansson!" I stated defiantly.

"Sounds like you're still angry."

"Why shouldn't I be angry? Everybody on the ship is angry the way he just deserted us. I don't understand why you aren't mad, Captain Bartlett."

"Me mad?" he questioned. "Being mad at Vilhjalmur for leavin' would make about as much sense as bein' mad at a dog for barkin'."

"I don't understand."

"A dog has ta bark. That's just its nature. An' men like Vilhjalmur have ta explore. He didn't travel halfway round the world ta sit on a hunk of ice. He had ta go."

"But how could he just abandon us and leave us in such danger!" I protested.

"I figure he thought we were safer than the danger he put himself inta. Ya have ta remember men like Stefansson, or Scott or Peary, aren't like most people. They're born for exploring. Take terrible chances with their lives ta reach new places an' see new things. An' they figure the rest of us are the same. He was just doin' what he figured needed ta be done."

"But—"

"But, nothing," he interrupted me. "Bein' angry doesn't help anybody. I was readin' some of the works of Confucius. You ever hear of him?"

I shook my head.

"He lived a long time ago…over a thousand years ago. He was a pretty smart old bird. He said bein' angry at somebody was like pickin' up a hot stone from a fire to throw at 'em. Whether ya hit 'em or not, ya still get yourself burned."

The music stopped again as the needle clicked repeatedly against the centre of the disc. Captain Bartlett picked up Figaro gently and placed him on my lap. He then rose from his chair to change the record. Without warning the ship shifted violently to the side. Figaro and I were thrown from my chair and the Captain fell against the gramophone. I felt my heart leap up into my chest and my eyes opened wide. Before I could say a word the ship pitched back the other way and I started to roll across the cabin. The air was filled with the sounds of crashing and tearing timber.

I felt a hand grab me by the arm and pull me to my feet. "It's time. Straight up and off the ship. Don't stop runnin' till your feet hit the ice."

17

I bounded across the floor, crossing the entire width of the cabin in two steps. I stopped at the door and looked back. Captain Bartlett had his back to me. He was bent over, in front of the remains of his record collection. What was he doing?

"Captain!" I called out.

He turned around and his eyes flamed. "Get movin', Helen! Off the ship! NOW!"

"You can't stay here! You've got to get off the ship too!"

"Course I do, lass! Ya think I'm fool enough ta go ta the bottom with this old girl? Get movin'. I got things ta do an' you're stoppin' me. Abandon ship. That's an order from your Cap'n!"

I turned and started running up the corridor. It was much darker. One of the lamps had been knocked off the wall and lay smashed on the floor. I could hear rushing water and pictured it flowing in through the gash in the side of the ship and filling the hold. There was a crash. The ship tilted violently to one side and I tumbled against the wall, and then fell to the floor, cushioning the fall with my hands and arms. I scrambled forward on all fours until I bumped my head against the base of the stairs. I pulled myself to my feet.

Wildly I started climbing up the stairs, desperate to

escape before it was too late. Then, along with the noise of the crashing timbers and rushing water, came another sound: music. When I reached the top of the stairs, I stopped. I peered back down the open hatch. The music got louder until it overwhelmed all the other sounds. Where was he? Why wasn't he coming?

Again the ship jerked violently and I would have fallen had I not been gripping the railing. I couldn't wait any longer. I raced out onto the deck. I could see people coming out on the ice, alerted by the sounds of the ship. I couldn't make out anybody, buried under parkas and hoods, but knew Mother and Michael would be amongst them. I didn't even want to think what Mother would say to me. I moved quickly along the deck, the music chasing me as I fled.

I reached the stairs and started down. A few people raced around the side of the ship and were waiting below, screaming out encouragement. I stumbled over my feet, almost regained my balance, and then fell face first, rolling down the last half-dozen steps.

"Helen, are ya all right?"

I looked up to see Jonnie standing over me.

"I'm fine," I mumbled. He helped me to my feet.

"EVERYBODY! GET BACK FROM THE SHIP! GET BACK! THE ICE IS GIVING!" somebody yelled.

"Come on, Helen, come on!"

"But Captain Bartlett's still on board!"

"Nothing we can do 'bout that. Come on," said Jonnie. Still holding me by the arm, he dragged me twenty or thirty paces away. We were surrounded by people.

"Helen! Helen!" I heard Mother scream. She threw her arms around me and squeezed hard.

"Mother, the Captain is still—"

"LOOK!" somebody yelled, "IT'S THE CAP'N!"

He'd come out of the same hatch as I had, but he was moving the wrong way! Rather than heading aft towards the stairs, he was racing to the front of the ship.

"Where is he going?" a voice asked.

No one answered. We all stood, wordlessly, frozen to the spot, following him with our eyes. It seemed as though the wind had stopped blowing and was holding its breath too, watching.

Even from this distance I could hear the music from the gramophone. It filled the air. I didn't know the name of the piece but I recognized it was Mozart, the Captain's favourite composer. The music was slow and solemn and dignified. Over the top of the music was the noise of bubbles surfacing from the hole in the side of the ship which was now below water level.

Captain Bartlett stopped mid-ship, and appeared to be fumbling with something.

"CAPTAIN!" I called out.

I tried to pull away from Mother but she held me firmly in her grip. I didn't struggle. Jonnie and Mr. Hadley and a few others left the huddle of people and moved across the ice. They stopped when they reached a spot close to the Captain.

"Please, we have to go closer," I said.

Mother released her grip on me. Michael ran beside me.

"What is he doing?" I asked, more to myself than to anybody else, but before the words left my mouth, I knew. He was standing beside the flag standard and he started to put up a flag. There was no wind and it hung limply. Hand over hand he raised it until it reached the top and then he tied it off. There was more wind at the top of the pole and it started to flutter gently. It was the Canadian Naval Ensign. Captain Bartlett stepped back a few steps and saluted the flag. Jonnie and other members of the crew on the ice did the same.

The ship seemed to be sinking faster. The air was bubbling out furiously and the deck was only a few feet above the surface of the ice. There was no possible way he could get down the stairs before it dipped below the surface of the water. It looked certain he'd be going down into the water.

"QUICK! SOMEBODY GET SOME LINES!" yelled Mr. Hadley.

A couple of men ran off towards the supply shelter.

Captain Bartlett started towards the stairs and then stopped and turned back to where we stood. He walked to the railing. His step wasn't hurried in any way. He reached into his coat and pulled out something—Figaro! He raised his arm and tossed the cat through the air. Figaro flew, turning end over end, black on top and white underneath, until she landed, feet first on the ice. Skidding and scrambling, she slid to a stop in a snowdrift.

My eyes went back to the Captain. He'd placed a foot on the bottom rung and started to climb the railing. He was coming over the side! He reached the very top of the railing. He grabbed hold of a piece of rigging to balance himself. The ship was going down fast and his head was not much higher than ours.

"JUMP! JUMP! JUMP!" somebody screamed.

There was a gap between the ship and the edge of the ice. If he didn't clear the gap he'd fall down into the water. I watched him bend at the knees, getting ready for the jump. He flew through the air, and seemed to hang there in mid-air. He hit the ice with a thud and rolled, stopping at our feet. Before anybody could even offer him a hand he bounded back to his feet. A couple of the men tried to say something but he shushed them and they fell silent.

Captain Bartlett turned to face the sinking ship. He pulled down the hood of his parka and removed his hat. Other people followed suit. We watched wordlessly. The only sounds were the escaping air and the strains of Mozart. The water washed over the deck and within seconds the railings and then the bridge disappeared beneath the surface, leaving only the masts and rigging still visible. The bubbles continued to rush to the surface, still carrying the notes of the symphony. Foot by foot the masts fell into the deep, faster and faster, until finally the tip of the tallest of the two, the flag waving briskly in the breeze, was all that was left. It seemed to pause, just for an instant, as though the flag was somehow going to stay above the water, and then it too plunged under the water and the *Karluk* was gone.

Everyone stood in stunned silence, staring at the place in the water where the ship had been trapped. It was now nothing more than a hole in the ice. Captain Bartlett took his hat and flung it into the hole. It floated for a few seconds and then began sinking below the surface, following the ship down.

"Mighty fine music, Cap'n," said Jonnie, breaking the trance. "What was it?"

"Mozart."

Despite everything I had to smile.

"The Funeral March. Thought it seemed fittin'. I always thought I'd have it played at my funeral." He stopped and smiled. "Bet some of ya thought that maybe taday was goin' ta be my funeral."

I burst into tears. Captain Bartlett wrapped an arm around me. "There, there, Helen," he said. "We can't have any tears. They might freeze ta your face."

He released his grip and smiled down at me. He walked over to the very edge of the ice and bent down. I trailed behind him. I stared down at the dark water. The water was already starting to freeze. Crystals were forming and joining together.

"Thirty minutes from now, there won't be any hole here. Less than an hour from that, it'll be thick enough ta walk on," Captain Bartlett noted. He stood up. "Helen, ya forgot something," he said as he reached into his parka. He pulled out my diary and put it in my hands.

"My diary!"

"After all the trouble ya went through ta get her, I couldn't let it go down ta the bottom."

I pressed it in close to my side.

"That is why you went back onto the ship?" Mother asked in a tone I knew and didn't like.

"Easy, Mrs. Kiruk. Nobody needs ta be angry at nobody. Have to excuse me, ladies...I'm tired...goin' ta go ta sleep...for a while."

As he walked away Figaro came scrambling across the ice after him.

18

"Mom! Helen!" Michael yelled as he crawled into our shelter.

I put aside my diary and Mother put down her sewing.

"The Captain's up. He wants us all to assemble in the centre of the shelters. He wants everybody there right away."

I was anxious to hear what he was going to say but disappointed I couldn't finish my journal entry. It had taken some effort to thaw the ink out by holding the bottle over the flame of a candle. The label had long since burned away and the glass bottle was blackened and smudged. We hurried out as quickly as possible.

Almost as soon as the *Karluk* had gone down, Captain Bartlett had gone to his shelter and to bed. He slept for almost twenty-four hours. A couple of the men, especially Dr. Murray and Dr. Mackay, had wanted him to answer questions, but Mr. Anderson wouldn't let them wake him. As first mate he was following the Captain's orders and those orders were for him not to be disturbed.

Jonnie told us how long the Captain had been up without sleep. He hadn't just been awake the previous night, supervising the dismantling of the ship, but the night before, listening to the sounds of the ice. He said the Captain figured the ship was going down but didn't see any reason to worry everybody when they couldn't do anything about it anyway.

We were amongst the last to assemble. It was almost noon and the moon shone brightly. There was an eerie yellow quality to the light, and shadows and edges seemed blurred and unfocused. As far as the eye could see the landscape was stark, barren ice, broken only by a small drift or a larger pressure ridge rising up. The winds were blowing strongly. With the *Karluk* gone there was nothing to break them as they roared down from the north.

"Can I have yer attention, please!" announced Captain Bartlett, and the crowd fell silent. "I took some readin's an' our position is latitude seventy-three degrees, ten minutes north, longitude, one hundred and sixty-five degrees an' five minutes west. Do those readin's correspond with the ones ya took yesterday, Dr. Murray?"

"Slight variations, but basically I concur with your findings."

"Thank ya, Doctor. As we sit here, the nearest land is ta the sou'-west. Wrangel Island sits about one hundred and twenty miles away. We'll be headin' for her."

"Wrangel Island! I'm familiar with it, Captain Bartlett," stated Henri Beauchat. "It is a chunk of rock and gravel thrown in the ocean. It is uninhabited. It supports little plant life and very few animals. What advantage is it to reach such an island?"

"Much of what ya say is correct, Mr. Beauchat. One clear advantage I see is that it is made up of rock an' gravel…things that aren't likely ta melt under our feet an' drop us inta the water below. An' while it's uninhabited, there is a whalin' outpost. Come whalin' season, ships'll be comin'."

"And when exactly would the ships arrive?" asked Dr. Mackay.

"May or June, dependin' on the ice."

"May or June! You do not honestly expect us to spend six or seven months on that island. Be reasonable, sir!" objected Dr. Murray.

"Seems reasonable ta me. Better there for six months than dead forever. Besides, what other choices do ya see?"

Dr. Murray and Dr. Mackay exchanged looks and then Dr. Murray stepped forward. "Since you asked, Captain, we do have an alternative plan."

"One that you and Dr. Mackay have been talkin' about?"

"Yes, along with others."

"Others?"

"Yes. Mr. Beauchat and Mr. Morrison."

"Mr. Morrison?" Captain Bartlett questioned.

Mr. Morrison stepped forward as well. "Yes, sir, Captain, sir. Meanin' no disrespect."

"None taken, Sandy. You're a good man. Let's hear the plan."

"We propose heading for Point Hope, on the Alaskan coast," Dr. Mackay said.

"Alaska! Point Hope is over three hundred miles away," Captain Bartlett replied loudly.

"Three hundred and twelve miles by my latest readings," countered Dr. Murray.

"That's a great distance. One I don't think that can be crossed."

"That is where you are wrong, Captain. As you all know, both Mr. Beauchat and I have previously travelled farther by dog sled."

"But that wasn't over shiftin' sea ice. Land doesn't buckle or break or let ya fall through. Besides, you'd be travellin' farther than that. Even if ya reached the Point ya'd still have over one hundred and fifty miles till ya reach a settlement."

"I have every confidence we can make it," Dr. Mackay said.

"Confidence is a good thing. I have one more question. How many dogs do ya suggest will accompany your party?"

"A full complement of course."

"An' how many would that be?"

"I don't know...I think we would have to sit down and discuss it...perhaps we can retire to your shelter and—" began Mr. Beauchat.

"No, sir, we won't be doin' that," Captain Bartlett interrupted. "Decisions affectin' all of us need ta be heard by all of us. How many dogs are ya suggestin'?"

"Ten or twelve animals," Dr. Murray responded, "and a sled and as many supplies as we can pack and carry."

Captain Bartlett nodded his head slowly. "A sled ya can have. Supplies are yours for the takin'. But dogs..." He turned to Kataktovick. "How many dogs do we have that are fit?"

Kataktovick didn't answer immediately. I would have been shocked if he had. He always thought through whatever he said.

"Thirty dogs...twenty-six for pulling...four for eating."

"About one dog for each of us. Four of ya goin' means you're entitled to four dogs."

"Four! That is ridiculous. We can't possibly make it with four dogs!" Mr. Beauchat replied angrily.

"Bett'r than the rest a us could make it with only the fourteen dogs ya'd be leaving us if ya took twelve with ya!" snapped Jonnie.

Captain Bartlett put a hand on Jonnie's shoulder.

"Sorry, Cap'n," he apologized.

"He raises an interesting point, Captain Bartlett," Dr. Murray began. "Whether you have fourteen or twenty-six dogs, you don't have enough to get all these people to Wrangel Island. Perhaps the key is to let us have all the dogs. We can make a run for it and send back help as soon as we reach a settlement."

"Send help back? Ya don't have ta do that," Captain Bartlett answered.

"We don't?"

"No sir, ya don't. No point in sending back help. By the time ya get there and help starts this way, there won't be anybody ta help. We'd all be dead, feedin' the fish."

"That is where you are wrong, Captain Bartlett. Giving us enough dogs to get there quickly is the only way we can get help to you in time."

"You're right about some things, Dr. Murray," said Captain Bartlett.

He is, I thought, and I could see by their expressions that others had the same thought.

"Yes, sir, ya's right about the number of dogs we need. We don't have near enough dogs ta get us all straight ta Wrangel. An' that's why we's goin' ta set up a number of shelters stocked with food an' fuel an' gear. Those shelters will be like steppin' stones…reachin' from here ta there. We're goin' ta use the dog teams ta mark a trail, set up an' stock the shelters. Same plan that got Peary ta the Pole. As ya know, the first of those shelters is already constructed. You've been ta it yourselves."

"And if we decide not to be part of this?" asked Dr. Mackay. "Are you going to deny us the right to pursue our plan?"

"Nope. Ya can go your own way an' all of us will be the worse for your decision. I was countin' on workin' all the dogs an' having the four of ya ta work the sleds. Can hardly afford ta lose men of your calibre."

"We were not wanting to hinder your plan, Captain, but simply to pursue ours. We think what we are suggesting is a better gamble," Mr. Beauchat declared.

"Gamble? Ha! Isn't any gamble about it. Those coming with me have a chance ta live. Those that don't …are dead."

Captain Bartlett spent most of the day trying to convince them it was better for everybody if they'd agree to be part of his plan. But they were as certain of their plan as he was of his. In the end they decided to leave. Dr. Murray, Dr. Mackay, Mr. Beauchat and Mr. Morrison would be heading out on their own, travelling towards Point Hope, Alaska. The Captain finally agreed they could take eight dogs—six healthy dogs and two of the others. They spent the remainder of the day packing up all the food and fuel and gear the sled could hold. They would leave in the morning.

In the dim morning light I peeked around one of the shelters and watched the four men make their final preparations. There were only six people standing around the sled, but I wasn't surprised there weren't more people. Mother couldn't bear to see them off; she said it was like watching somebody digging their own grave. Jonnie told me he didn't want to say goodbye to anybody "that was stealin' huskies we'd be needing."

He thought they were traitors for not following the Captain's orders and he intended to stay inside his shelter so he wouldn't say anything he shouldn't.

"Who's there?" asked Michael, peering around my shoulder.

"I'm not sure…I can't tell under the parkas," I answered. I knew what he wanted to know: was the Captain there. I didn't think so but I didn't want to say.

The men worked hooking up the dogs, loading the sled and checking the ties. The dogs snapped and snarled at each other, as if they were edgy or maybe realized what was going to soon begin. I was pleased to see Daisy wasn't amongst the dogs they were taking. Michael had assured me there was no way Kataktovick would let them take her but I needed to see it with my own eyes to believe it. On the ground, beside the sled, lay four backpacks.

I looked off into the dim, thin light in the distance. Somewhere beyond the horizon, a small dot on a map hundreds of miles away was their destination.

"Ya come ta see us off, have ya?"

I was startled to see Sandy Morrison standing directly in front of me.

I nodded my head, but found I couldn't look into his eyes. I stared down at the ice.

"Why don't you an' your brother come on over and say your goodbyes. I was 'oping the Cap'n would be 'ere…but I guess not…. Can't blame 'im none," Mr. Morrison said with reservation.

He walked back towards the sled and we followed behind him. As we walked I gazed off into the distance again. I stopped in my tracks and cupped my hands over my eyes. I thought I saw something out on the horizon. I rubbed my eyes. Sometimes the shadows hit the ice at strange angles and things seem to appear. It's like mirages in the desert.

I looked back, expecting it to be gone, but it was still there, just a tiny bit bigger. I watched, transfixed. The dot got bigger and bigger and became two dots and then three, and then a whole bunch. It was crazy but it looked like ... I could hardly bring myself to think the words ... a sled and team.

"He's coming back," I said.

"What?" asked Michael.

I turned to him in shock. I hadn't even realized I'd spoken the words out loud. I pointed my hand and Michael's eyes followed my arm out into the distance.

"What?" he asked again.

I wanted to answer him. To tell him he was coming back for us. That Mr. Stefansson was coming to rescue us, but I said nothing, just kept pointing. It was just like in the dreams I still had at night—visions of him returning for us ... that he hadn't really abandoned us ... that we'd all be safe ...

"LOOK!" I heard Mr. Morrison yell, and all heads turned in the direction I was already pointing.

We all stood and stared as the dots became so large and clear there was no doubt. Two men were running and taking turns on the back of a sled pulled by more than a dozen huskies.

"It's him!" Mr. Morrison said. "It's the Cap'n."

"What?" I asked.

"Cap'n Bartlett an' somebody else," Mr. Morrison said.

"Kataktovick," Michael added. "I can tell by the way he lopes along as he runs."

They closed the last two hundred yards quickly. The dogs knew their breakfast would be waiting when they stopped. Captain Bartlett pulled hard on the reins and brought the team to a stop. He climbed off the back of the sled and walked into our midst as Kataktovick led the sledge away.

"Good day, gentlemen…young Helen and Michael."

People returned greetings.

"I was hoping ta get here before ya started. I think ya won't be needin' them packs ta be so full," he said, motioning to the ground.

"What do you mean?" asked Mr. Beauchat sharply. "We need every ounce we can carry!"

"You are not reneging on your word, are you, sir?" Dr. Murray's voice was filled with indignation.

"Ya can stop right now, ya can!" Mr. Morrison stated angrily. "The Cap'n is a man of his word. 'Ear 'im out!"

"Thank ya, Mr. Morrison. Ya won't be needin' ta fill your packs because a cache of supplies is waitin' for ya. Red flag, up on top of an ice shelter. Twenty… maybe twenty-one miles along your route."

"But…how?" Dr. Murray asked.

"Me and Kataktovick marked a trail. Red flags, about every half-mile. Follow 'em. Had ta swing ta the north ta get around a big pressure ridge. Clear, fast ice. Took us longer ta blaze the trail. Faster ta get back. Ya should make the shelter in six…maybe eight hours."

"Captain, I don't know what to say…" Dr. Murray began.

"I do," Mr. Morrison interjected. "Thanks, Cap'n."

"No need for thanks, Mr. Morrison. Words in the good book, 'do unto others,' is all."

Mr. Beauchat stepped forward. He pulled down his hood and removed his right glove, exposing his hand. He reached out his arm to the Captain. Captain Bartlett removed his glove and they shook hands. Dr. Murray and Dr. Mackay followed right after. When it came to Mr. Morrison, he and the Captain reached out their hands and then came together in a hug.

Mr. Morrison lingered beside the Captain, close to where Michael and I stood, while the other three returned to the sled.

"Cap'n, sir, I was hopin' ya could do me a favour."

"Course, Mr. Morrison. What is it I can do?"

Mr. Morrison reached into the pocket of his parka and pulled something out. It was small and white and he pressed it quickly into the Captain's hands. Captain Bartlett brought it up to his face and I could see it was a letter.

"Could ya...could ya make sure me mother gets this," he asked.

Captain Bartlett nodded and placed the letter in his pocket. I looked at Michael. He looked as confused as I felt.

Within minutes they were standing beside the sled, their now partially unloaded packs on their backs. A light snow had started to fall and the wind was picking up. At least the wind was at their backs and it might push them along. A few other people had come out onto the ice. They gathered around where the Captain and Michael and I stood, and not too close to the four men and their sled. It was as though they were doing something personal, or private, and we didn't want to intrude.

Finally Dr. Murray looked at us and raised a hand to his head, almost in a salute.

"God be with ya!" Captain Bartlett yelled out.

They turned and started to move. One man took to the back of the sled while the other three started trudging beside it. We watched them get smaller and smaller and the yapping of the dogs faded away, captured by the falling snow. I could see them for a good five minutes, getting smaller and smaller until they vanished.

"Captain, why did Mr. Morrison give you a letter for his mother?" asked Michael.

I wanted to ask the same question, but didn't think it was polite to do so.

"'Cause he wants her ta know what became of him."

"I don't understand," I said.

"He doesn't figure they're goin' ta make it, but figures we will."

"Then why…why did he go with them? Why didn't he stay with us?" Michael asked.

"'Cause he told 'em he'd go. They've been talkin' for awhile. He got himself all caught up in the plan an' he gave his word. A man who doesn't keep his word isn't much of a man…and Mr. Morrison is a man of his word."

"Even if it means dying?" Michael asked incredulously.

"Especially if it means dying. Anybody can keep his word if it doesn't cost him nothin'. Only a man of true honour will keep his word in the face of death. Not much more important than your honour. Ya'll learn that some day, Michael. Ya'll learn."

19

Dear Diary,

The light snow which started to blow when the party set out on their own got stronger and stronger and stronger. It didn't stop the first day, or the next, or the next or the next. Kataktovick said they'd be okay if they just sat tight in the shelter he and the Captain had made for them. I just hoped they got there before the storm closed in.

For the past four days I couldn't even see the distance between our ice shelter and the next one, even though it's no more than two dozen paces between the two. It was only by keeping a hand on the lines linking the shelters we were even able to get around.

It seemed the longer the storm raged the smaller the shelters became. We had to stay inside except for short trips between the igloos, or outside to relieve ourselves...always holding those lines tightly. Lose the line and you could lose your life.

The Captain had told us about a man who stumbled out into an Arctic storm and got lost. He described how panicked and confused he

*would have become; how he would have lost all
sense of direction, unable to see beyond the tip
of his nose in the driving snow; how he desper-
ately would have stumbled around, falling to his
knees and trying to feel his way back to his shelter; how they found him the next morning when
the storm finally broke, frozen to death, curled
up in a little ball, just five paces from his shelter.*

He told us that story five different times. I'd
never heard him repeat a story before. I think he
was trying to scare us into staying inside or on
the lines. For me, he was just wasting his time. I
was already so scared the first time I heard the
story that it kept on replaying in my mind, even
haunting me in my sleep. What a terrible way to
die.

Being forced to stay inside for so long, we
found ways to pass the time. The chess games,
which had been so much a part of life on
the ship, continued. There was almost always a
couple of games going on in the shelter where
Cookie had set up his portable stove. I liked
playing chess. When I first started playing,
everybody was always willing to help me. Not
now. I was winning sometimes, and they weren't
so helpful.

Michael didn't like chess. He spent a lot of
time playing a game that Kataktovick and the
other Inuit played called Knuckle Bones. It's just
like playing with a ball and jacks except they
used bones, real knuckle bones. Most of the
crew had started playing and gambling on the
games, but the Captain put a stop to it. He said
gambling was a sin against God and it wasn't

wise to ever do anything to make God upset, but especially when you're marooned on the ice.

I was very glad when he stopped the gambling. Something about it seemed to bring out the worst in the men. Arguments were always breaking out, and on two occasions, these developed into shoving matches. Others had stepped in and stopped them before they got out of hand, but it was so distressing to witness. The Captain had threatened he wouldn't tolerate any more fisticuffs, and that we should all be saving our fight for the real enemy.

I knew the men weren't just upset about the matchsticks they lost in the gambling games. Ever since the ship had gone down tempers had flared. Good-natured humour was as hard to come by as warmth. People argued about almost anything and even close friends didn't seem as close. Mother said spirits would improve once we were moving again. I think she was right. The hardest part was waiting. It left too much time to think about what we had to do.

Mr. Hadley still spent a great deal of time playing Knuckle Bones. He was spending more and more time with the Inuit, especially Kataktovick. For somebody who said they were all "dirty, dishonest, lazy Indians," he sure acted friendly and treated them well. Maybe he was seeing things differently now.

Anyway, I had thought it was pretty awful, playing with bones like that. Then Jonnie pointed out to me that my chess pieces, the ones the Captain gave me, are made of ivory. Elephant tusks are really just elephant bones.

Besides reading my books over and over again, I spent a great deal of time listening to the stories which continued to be told, now around a table in the biggest of the ice shelters. The Inuit stories are interesting but eerie and scary and confusing. I guess partly it's because of the language problems. Kataktovick's English is getting better all the time but lots of words are lost in the translation. The stories are all about the animals and the weather and ice. Hearing them tell these stories made the north seem less lonely. Even when there aren't any living things, there are still the spirits filling the air and ice. Unfortunately some of those spirits don't seem very nice.

Of course you can't just sit and listen to other people's stories without telling some of your own. I didn't think I had any stories to contribute until Michael suggested I retell the stories I'd read. Once I started to do that, and after I got over being so nervous, I had lots to tell. The men seemed to like my stories.

Sometimes the Captain was there to listen. That made me nervous all over again. He liked my stories, especially those that take place way down south where the weather was always warm and sunny. He said it helped him to keep warm and...

I shook the pen to try to force a little more ink out of it. The ink in the bottle had continued to get thicker and thicker and was now just a frozen mass. If I wanted to continue I'd have to reheat the bottle. I decided to finish later. The storm was subsiding and I wanted to go outside. I closed my diary. One of the few good things about the cold was that the ink dried the instant it was set on the page. I lifted up one of the covers on my bed and tucked the diary inside. Figaro, sleeping at the bottom of the bed, opened one eye and then stretched. I reached over and scratched him behind one of his ears and he pressed his head against my hand. He'd spent all of the last four days in our shelter and I hoped the Captain didn't miss him too much.

Coming out of the entrance tunnel I was pleased to see the storm was almost over and it seemed to have left behind some light. In the sky, just barely above the horizon was the sun, as if it wanted to peek out and see everything was still all right. It was the same fiery ball I remembered, but it sent down no heat to warm away the chill from the air or the ache in my bones. I just stood there and watched it for a full fifteen minutes until it dropped out of sight and the eerie twilight returned. It had been up in the sky for less than thirty minutes.

Then I remembered what Captain Bartlett had said to us at that first meeting: "We're goin' ta make a run for it. Have ta go when the sun returns ta light the way, but before it burns off the ice and drops us inta the ocean."

It was time for us to leave.

Mother had been in charge of making the flags, which, of course, meant Michael and I had worked along with her. We'd started making them before the ship went down. In all we'd made almost two hundred and fifty of them. I knew the number well. Two flags for every mile of ice. Two hundred and fifty flags for one hundred and twenty-five miles of ice. They were small red

triangles of material attached to wooden stakes. They
were much taller than me but once they were driven
into the ice the flag at the top would be level with my
head.

When we first started working on them I found the
job tedious and boring. Then, once it was explained
how important these flags were, I worked more intently.
They would be our path markers to safety and had to
be strong and secure enough to ensure that no storm
could rip it from the pole. The poles would guide us.

I grabbed an armful of flags and pushed them down
the incline of the tunnel and out of the ice shelter ahead
of me. I slid out after them. Michael walked back,
empty-handed. He'd already dropped off some of the
flags.

"Give me a hand," I ordered.

"Why should I?"

"Because I'm your older sister and I'm telling you to
help."

"Not good enough," he smirked.

I picked up one of the poles. "Because if you don't
obey me I just might take one of these poles and smack
your bottom with it."

"You wouldn't … and besides it hardly would hurt
through all my clothes."

"I would … and I guess we'll find out," I answered.

Michael quickly bent down and grabbed one of the
poles. I wasn't sure whether he was going to help or try
to hit me with it. He bent down again and grabbed a
second and a third and a fourth. I gathered up the rest.
We carried them to where the sleds were being loaded.

They were using the sleds Mother had helped to
build—the komatiks. They were both loaded down
with supplies. The poles were being added and then the

entire load would be tied in place under skins. I counted the dogs...seven...hooked up to each sled. Daisy was the lead dog for one of the teams. The dogs were mostly just lying on the ice, waiting.

"Here they are, Jonnie," I said, handing him my handful of poles. Mr. Hadley took the others out of Michael's arms and they divided them between the two sleds.

As they started to tie things down my attention was caught by the Captain. He wasn't far away. He was holding his sextant, gazing through it to figure out our location and the direction we'd need to be travelling. Up here, so close to the magnetic north pole, the compass was almost useless so they'd be guided by his readings. If he was out by even a few degrees we'd never find the island, or at best, would have to travel much farther to finally get there.

The Captain would be leading the first team. He had told me he needed to make sure these first few legs were completely accurate and he wanted to take the sextant readings along the route. With him would go Jonnie and Kataktovick. I wished Jonnie wasn't going; I liked talking to him.

Today they'd travel to the ice shelters where I spent my overnight. From there they were going to cover between twenty and thirty miles, marking the trail with the flags. At the farthest point they'd build more shelters.

About twelve hours after the original group left, a second party would head out. This party, led by Mr. Hadley, would follow the flags towards the waiting shelters. Even though they'd be much more heavily loaded down with supplies, they'd be able to travel more quickly because of the trail created by the first team.

The two parties would meet at the shelters and spend the night. In the morning one party, carrying supplies and flags, would set out to mark the next part of the trip. The other group would leave almost all their supplies and gear at the shelters and return to camp. These supplies would be used later, when we all started our journey. The returning party could travel fast because of the lighter load, but if they were delayed by a storm, they would only have enough food or fuel to survive for a few days. This was part of the gamble.

Before the second party had returned to the camp, a third would set out. They'd meet the returning party somewhere along the route. This third group would be made up of six men. They'd have to be strong because they, and not dogs, would be pulling one of the two large sleds weighed down with food. They'd leave their entire load at the first set of shelters and return to camp.

Closing my eyes I tried to picture what they would be doing; how it was going to be there on the ice; how lonely it would be; and most important, how it would feel to be out there myself. I knew it would be different than on the short overnight trip. In just a few days I'd find out just how different.

20

I turned and shifted on my cot. I couldn't get to sleep. I could hear the soft breathing of Mother and Michael, asleep just off to my side. Mother was whistling a little with each breath. The only other sound was the ever-present wind outside stirring up the snow. It wasn't blowing hard, just hard enough for me to hear it through the walls.

My thoughts continually turned to the men out on the ice. There were fourteen of them, in three groups, out there, somewhere. I was sure they were all headed back towards our camp now. It had been eight days since the Captain left. Just before he started he'd told me it would take them between seven and ten days to set up the first three "stepping stones." After completing them, they'd all return to camp, rest for a day, and then we'd all leave.

The camp had become my safe haven in the same way the ship had…well, at least before it sank. I knew we couldn't stay here, but I was afraid to leave. And when they returned, I knew we'd soon be gone.

"Helen…" Michael called out.

"What?"

"I gotta go."

"Go where?" I asked vacantly.

"You know, outside, to relieve myself."

"Now? Can't you wait?"

"No," he quietly moaned.

"All right," I said reluctantly. "But sssshhhhh! We don't want to wake Mother."

She'd been having trouble sleeping for the past week and had taken some sleeping powder before going to bed this evening. Dr. Mackay had given her some in the first weeks of the trip and she'd saved one dose.

It was pitch black in the shelter and both Michael and I had to get up and feel our way to the tunnel. He was already there by the time I'd worked my way over. I pushed aside the curtain and slid down the incline after him.

The moon was nearly full and was high in the sky. Its light bounced off the ice and provided just enough light for us to see. It was funny how the darkness seemed so much more heavy and frightening ever since a little daylight had come back. I didn't like to be outside at night any more. Somehow darkness at twelve midnight was more scary than darkness at twelve noon.

Each day, the sun stayed up in the sky for fifteen minutes longer than the day before. Yesterday it appeared at just after ten in the morning and didn't dip below the horizon until almost two in the afternoon.

There was a light frosting of snow being blown around and it whipped up into my face as I trudged after Michael. It stung my cheeks so I dipped my face down. There was always snow blowing around up here but it rarely "fell." I'd learned that although we were on the ice in the middle of an ocean we were also in the middle of a "desert." There was as much precipitation here each year as in the Sahara Desert.

"Hey!" exclaimed Michael as I bumped into him.

"Sorry," I said, and moved backwards a step.

He turned to face me. "Do you mind?"

"Mind? Mind what?"

"I wanted you to come out here with me...not stand right beside me. Could I have a little privacy?"

"Certainly, your highness!"

I walked away five or six steps, back towards the camp. I turned around. I didn't know where his modesty was coming from but I understood what he meant about some privacy. We were all in such close quarters there was almost no place to just be by yourself. We were the only people for hundreds of miles in any direction, but we were all trapped together in the ice shelters. Looking back at the camp the blowing snow was now at my back and it suddenly felt less cold and harsh.

There were over a dozen different-sized shelters. The light reflecting off the ice gave an eerie glow which highlighted the buildings and caused them to throw long shadows stretching almost out to where I stood. The flag flapped away noisily and the line pinged against the pole. It was almost beautiful.

Some of the shelters were filled with life; people were inside, sleeping. But others, more than half of them, were empty. The men who would have filled them were still out on the ice.

I reached into my pockets to get my gloves but of course they weren't there. At night I always used them as a pillow and they were still inside on my bunk. I was always forgetting to take them outside.

"Hurry up, Michael," I said, looking around.

"I'm trying. It's hard to rush with all these layers of clothes on."

"Try harder, I'm getting cold and..." I stopped in mid-sentence. My eyes had caught a blur of movement—a flash of grey. I looked hard. There was nothing, nothing at all. It had to be just a trick of the light coming in across the ice.

Then something caught my eye again. Movement, and then nothing. I tried to stare through the darkness. Everything was just different shades of grey. I stared harder.

"What ya staring at?" Michael asked. He had finished and was right behind me.

I almost jumped into the air.

"What's wrong?"

"Ssshhhhhh," I hissed at him. "I think there's something there."

"Yeah…some igloos." He started walking. "Come on, let's get back to the shelters. It's cold and I want to…" He stopped a dozen steps ahead of me.

We both saw it at the same instant. It looked like a big, shaggy, oversized dog as it moved slowly and deliberately, lumbering from behind one of the shelters, its nose to the ground. In the dim light it didn't seem white, just a darker shade of grey. It lifted its head and swung it back and forth, from side to side, like it was trying to find something.

I remembered the stories Kataktovick had told about polar bears. The polar bear, or Nanook, was a big part of their myths and lives. He had said they couldn't see very well. In the dim light, with all the shades of grey, they could only pick out things that moved. Of course, anyone or any animal seeing a polar bear would try to run away. To make up for their poor sight, they possess an incredible sense of smell. That was why the Captain wouldn't let us bring food into any of the shelters except the cook house.

There was one other thought that kept spinning around inside my head: polar bears think of people the same way they think of a seal or walrus or deer or fish, just another source of food.

The bear continued to swing its head around. I could see the nostrils flaring and realized it was smelling the air, trying to "see" with its nose. We'd be okay as long as we were downwind of the bear. Downwind ... my heart sank. We were directly upwind. Walking away from the camp the snow had been blowing right into our faces, back into our tracks. Now the wind was blowing right past us to where the bear stood.

"Helen, it's..." Michael started to say.

"SSSHHH!" I hissed loudly. Too loudly. The bear turned around and stared directly at where we stood. It knew something was out there, but wasn't exactly sure where. The bear took a few steps forward and then stopped. It made a low hissing sound, like a cat or a snake. I shuddered. I knew what the bear was doing. It was trying to make the invisible prey move.

I heard Michael quietly whimpering. I prayed the sound hadn't reached the bear. The bear took two more tentative steps towards us and stopped. It opened and closed its jaws repeatedly, and I could hear the sound of the teeth chomping together. Again it hissed, this time louder and longer. Almost in answer, Michael whimpered. It stared straight ahead, straight at us, but still I prayed it didn't see us.

I knew this couldn't go on for much longer. It was stalking us, coming closer and closer. Soon, in a few more seconds or a few more feet, we would come into focus and the bear would charge. Michael would panic and start running and the bear would chase him down and...I stopped. What if it wasn't Michael who moved? The bear growled, a full, long, loud, throaty cry that almost drove my plan from my mind.

"Michael, stay still," I said quietly. "Whatever happens...don't move until the bear has gone. Do you understand?"

"Yes," his voice croaked.

The bear cocked its massive head to one side, aiming an ear at our voices. It still gazed in our direction with one eye, a black hole against the grey of its head. I moved, just slightly off to one side. The bear stopped dead in its tracks. Terrified, I fought the urge to simply freeze again. I had to move. I shuffled sideways another step. The bear, still not moving, swivelled its head to follow my motion. It growled again. This time it was different. Much more quiet. I imagined it was a sigh of satisfaction, like: "I've got you now." I shuffled over another step, and then another and another.

I turned back towards Michael. "Don't move until you know it's not after you."

He nodded.

Then I ran.

I heard the bear groan and the sound of scraping, its claws digging into the ice as it leaped forward. I ran off to the side, trying somehow to angle around the bear and reach the far side of the camp. Out of the corner of my eye, I could see the bear. It was charging towards me in big loping strides, quickly closing the gap between us. I screamed uncontrollably! It was getting bigger and bigger, coming closer and closer. I could see every ripple of its body, the muscles, the folds of the skin, the mouth partly open, the thick tongue hanging out of one side. It was like slow motion, as if the bear was running through deep water. I could see every detail but none of it seemed real. I stopped screaming and, unexplainably, started laughing. It was as though I was watching it from a distance, as if there was no danger. There was a wave of relief as I realized the bear couldn't possibly get me because I was no longer there. My body got warm all over and I felt myself just melt. I fell to the ice.

The thud brought me back to reality, but within a split second I felt a crushing blow against my back. I raised my head just high enough off the ground to see the bear rolling, head over tail. It slid to a stop. It had tripped over me when I dropped to the ice. It shook its massive head and turned and faced me. I tried to sit up but couldn't catch my breath. My chest hurt and I thought I was going to pass out. The bear snarled and came forward once more until it was just a few short strides away. It was in no rush. It knew I had no escape. The beast rose up on its hind legs and I gasped. A mass of white fur, blotting out the horizon and stretching up to the sky, soared over me. And then I saw a huge paw coming towards me.

21

I tried to sit up. A groan escaped my lips.

"Helen, you're okay! Praise the Lord!"

I turned towards Mother's voice.

"Don't try to get up!" she said as she rushed over and eased my shoulders back onto the cot.

"What happened?" I asked weakly. My chest hurt and my head was spinning around. "What happened... the bear?"

"It's dead... shot dead."

"But how... who?" I asked, forcing the words out.

"Kataktovick heard you screaming. He shot it as it was starting to swing at you. Then it collapsed, on top of you. Oh Helen, we were so worried... I was so scared I was going to lose my daughter as well..."

She started to cry and wrapped her arms around me. My chest hurt badly and I needed her to loosen her grip, but not as much as I needed her arms around me. Finally she released me and looked into my eyes.

"Michael told me... he told us all, what you did. Helen, that was so brave, so very brave."

I nodded weakly and felt my eyes start to close.

"It's going to be okay, Helen. Go to sleep."

The curtain parted and a head poked through the tunnel. I was surprised to see it was Kataktovick. He was one of the last people I expected to come in here. He was always friendly enough, but he never said a word to me unless I asked him something. He nodded his head and smiled and came to the side of my cot. I slid my feet out of the sack and sat up.

"Hello, Kataktovick. Thank you for what you did."

He nodded his head. I waited for him to speak but he didn't. I needed to break the silence. "I guess I was lucky you came along right at that time or I would have been killed."

"There a while."

"You were there a while? Why didn't you shoot it sooner?"

"Bad shot. Had to wait to not hit Helen. Also watch to see if bear change to Inuit."

"What do you mean? I don't understand?"

"Bear sometimes changes to man. Sometimes man changes to bear." He held out his hand. "Take." I reached out and he dropped something into my hand. It was a tooth.

"From bear."

I turned it over, looking at it carefully. It was unbelievably long and smooth to the touch, snowy white all the way down to the yellow root. I was holding in my hand one of the teeth that would have crushed me to death.

"Atagtat...wear around neck."

"Around my neck? Like a charm?"

"Protect...safe...powerful. Helen okay?" he asked.

"I guess so. I'm just very tired."

"Tired, yes. I been pleadin' ta tupilaks," he said.

"Tupilaks? What is a tupilak?"

"Ummm, tupilaks..." I could tell he was struggling to find the word in English. He smiled. "Spirits."

"Thank you, but you don't have to plead to the spirits for me. I'm fine, really."

"Not you...for white one."

"White one?"

"Yep. White one. One without a shadow."

"For the bear?"

He nodded.

"You're praying for the bear!"

He nodded again. "Took life of bear...need to plead with tupilaks...spirits...to make the bones get covered with meat again...make bear come back."

"I don't understand."

Kataktovick looked more confused by me not understanding than I was by his story.

"Plead with spirits...pray...for five days after bear killed...if don't...bear never return."

He turned around and walked to the highest part of the domed ceiling. He raised his hands into the air and started to chant.

It was a strange, haunting cry. I listened, mesmerized, as he continued to chant. Soon I detected a pattern. It wasn't Mozart, but it had that same haunting sort of quality. I stood up. I found myself quietly humming along to the melody.

Kataktovick turned to me and smiled. He continued to chant and I joined in, the best I could manage.

22

The blowing snow had kept us trapped in our shelters for three days after the last party, led by the Captain, returned to the camp. The Captain had wanted to leave the day after his return, taking just enough time to load up all the sleds and go. I could tell, without him saying anything, that he was impatient. I knew part of the reason we hadn't left was the weather. But the other reason was me; they feared I wasn't well enough to move. At first my chest ached with each breath and I had a terrible headache. These pains passed. Mother had me check closely to make sure I wasn't leaking blood out of either end. I prayed to God each night and gave thanks each morning when no blood came. Mr. Hadley said the force of the bear had only "bent" my ribcage and "rang" my bell. There weren't even any cuts on my back. My thick clothing, which had gotten shredded by the bear's claws, had protected me. Mother had stitched up the rips so well they weren't even noticeable.

I heard the sound of somebody coming in through the tunnel. I swung my feet off the cot and got to my feet gingerly. The curtain was pushed aside and Michael's parka-covered head came through.

He looked up at me. "It's time," he said quietly. "Are you ready?"

"Of course I'm ready," I snapped back, and then

instantly regretted speaking so sharply. He'd been very nice to me since the bear attack. He hadn't teased me or made fun of me in days. Mother had said this would probably end soon, so I should enjoy it while it lasted. I almost missed him giving me a hard time. Almost.

Kataktovick and the other Inuit had also been acting differently around me. They were treating me like I wasn't a child any more; they were more quiet and serious. I knew the Inuit had great respect and fear for Nanook, the polar bear, and I'd faced him. Kataktovick said they'd be telling my story to their families when they returned and these stories would live on longer than we would. That was a strange thought; something I'd done would be told and retold by people I'd never meet and would never know. Strange, but nice. Like being a character…a hero…in a novel.

"Helen…"

"Yeah, I'm coming, I'm coming."

"No…I just…I just wanted to ask you a question."

I turned around and looked at him. "Sure, what?"

"I wanted to know why."

"Why what?" I asked.

"Why did you do it…have the bear chase after you? Why didn't you just stand there?"

"I don't know. You're my brother. Wouldn't you have done the same thing for me?"

Michael looked sheepish but didn't answer.

"Wouldn't you have?"

"I don't know, maybe," he answered. "I always thought I'd be the one doing something like that, but I was so scared I couldn't do anything."

"I was scared too," I admitted.

"But you did something. I just didn't expect it… didn't expect you to be the one saving me…it was just…

just so unlike you. Why did you do it?"

I would have been offended by what he said if I hadn't agreed. It wasn't like me.

Over the past few days, lying there on my bed, waiting for the storm to break, I'd tried to answer the same question. I kept thinking back to Father. All through his sickness he'd gotten smaller and smaller. He became weaker, hardly able to hold his head up. I sat and watched helplessly through the weeks which stretched into months. I knew there was nothing I could do for Father except witness his death. And, out on that ice, facing the polar bear, I knew I couldn't simply watch another member of my family die.

Michael stood waiting for an answer I couldn't really give him yet. "We better get going," I said. Michael retreated out of the tunnel.

I started to tighten up the buttons and clasps of my parka and then pulled on my mitts. Slowly I looked around the shelter and at Mother's large trunk. It was to be left. It contained all the clothing we didn't have on our bodies or on the sleds. The clothes were folded and mended. Only Mother would be so neat with clothing destined for the bottom of the ocean. There was space on the sleds for food, fuel and our survival gear, but not for much more. We each had a little space for personal things and I'd packed my diary and chess set.

I picked up the oil lamp and carried it over to the tunnel. I placed it on the ice and then dropped to my knees and started to back out through the opening. I reached to extinguish the lamp, and then stopped. This lamp wasn't coming with us. I dimmed the flame, and it cast a soft, gentle light which illuminated the curves of the shelter. The scene was peaceful and calm. Anyone coming here would find it inviting. I knew it didn't make any sense, because nobody would be coming, but it made me feel better. I wanted to remember it as a safe and friendly place.

The rush of brilliant white light blinded me as I stood up. The sun was low in the sky, just above the horizon. It didn't really rise very high in the sky ever. It just circled around the horizon. Its light, coming at us flat across the open ice, bounced off all the ice and snow, and was dazzlingly bright. There wasn't a cloud in the sky. I slipped on my snow goggles, which were specially made to block out some of the sun's rays. We would have almost six hours of brilliant sunlight and without the goggles my eyes would be damaged. Snow blindness can happen to anybody who travels without protection over the snow in bright sunlight for a long time.

Clouds of vapour came out of our mouths and rose straight into the air before vanishing. There was a slight wind but it couldn't push away my breath or penetrate through my thick clothing. I guessed it was probably no more than twenty degrees below zero. I pulled down my hood and felt the air sting my ears. I quickly pulled the hood back up. Shielding my eyes with my hand, I looked around.

Everybody in the camp had already assembled outside the shelters. The twenty-one dogs lay quietly on the ice, divided into teams. Two teams of four dogs each were harnessed to the two komatiks. Three dogs, unfit for pulling, were simply tied to the side, and the remaining ten dogs were divided into two teams and harnessed to the two larger sleds. All four sledges were piled high with supplies, covered by canvas. These supplies were everything we'd need for the next four or five months, not just on the ice but for our stay on the island while we were waiting for the whalers to come ashore. The Captain said we could hope for some game once we made it to shore, but we wouldn't have any time to spend hunting while we were on the ice.

I walked over and rubbed Daisy behind the ears. She nuzzled against me, finding the pocket holding the treat. I removed the biscuit and held it flat on my hand. She gobbled it down hungrily. I didn't think it was right she should have to pull the sled since she was expecting puppies. She didn't look any different to me under all her thick fur but Kataktovick said she was pretty far along.

Next I went to check on Figaro. I pulled aside a cover from one of the large sleds. His container, a small wooden box, was securely anchored in place. I flipped the latch open and reached in quickly before he could get out.

"It's all right," I said, stroking him with the hand that wasn't pinning him in place.

His ears were flattened down and his tail whipped back and forth angrily.

"I don't know why you're so upset. You're the only one who doesn't have to walk," I said.

I pushed against him and slipped my hand out of the container, relatching it. He'd be fine in there…unless of course the sled went through the ice. But that was no different than for any of us.

The two smaller komatiks started to move. I heard the cry of the men driving the dogs forward and watched as the animals, two komatiks and six men took off across the ice. They were going on ahead. Their goal was to reach the first shelter, drop off their supplies and come back to help take part of our loads. I watched them until they disappeared into the distance.

I was always struck by how big the Arctic was, how it could just swallow somebody up and make them vanish.

"How ya doin' taday, Helen?"

I turned around. "I'm fine, sir. How are you?"

Captain Bartlett smiled and chuckled softly. "It wasn't me dancin' with a polar bear. How's the ribs? How's your breathin'?"

"Everything's fine, sir, no problem at all," I lied, not wanting him to know I still felt a tenderness. I wasn't exactly sure why I didn't want people to know I still wasn't completely right yet. I guess in part I was afraid to tell the Captain, thinking that maybe he'd delay things until I was more ready, and knowing we couldn't afford to wait any longer.

I also remembered one of the stories Mr. Hadley had told us about how the Inuit abandon the old and dying on the ice. I had terrible illogical thoughts that if I was too sick to go on, I could be left behind to die.

The Captain walked towards the two sleds and everybody who had been scattered or talking fell silent. We stood around him on all sides. He pulled back his hood to reveal a tangle of dark hair, tinged with streaks of grey. There had been no grey when we set sail from Vancouver.

"Can we all bow our heads for a prayer," he said softly.

The men tipped back their hoods and removed their hats. We all bowed our heads.

"Dear God up in heaven. I want ta thank ya for the blessin's ya have provided for us all. Ta thank ya for keepin' us safe an' warm an' protected in your love an' for grantin' us this test of our faith. I pray that ya be with us in our journey across the ice like ya was for the children of Israel in their travels through the desert an' that we too can find the promised land. Amen."

"Amen," we echoed back. Hats and hoods were repositioned to protect us from the cold. I picked up a lead and tied it to my waist. At the Captain's request, Mother had made a series of leather leads that would be attached to the sleds. We would use these to harness ourselves to the sleds in order to pull the loads. We all had to help because there was too much weight and not enough dogs to do the work.

"Helen!" the Captain called. I looked up at him. "Untie the lead. You're ta walk here beside me."

"But everybody has to pull!"

He fixed me with an angry, evil eye, and I regretted speaking back to him. I pulled off my gloves and clumsily tried to undo the knot. He walked over and finished untying the lead.

"Ya have ta listen ta your Captain, lassie."

I blinked back tears. "I just want to help, like everybody else."

"Everybody else wasn't squashed like a bug by a bear. Understand?"

I nodded.

"Good, good. Now, I just want ya ta stay close beside me. Tell me one of your stories ... maybe one about the South Seas or some such place. It'll make the travellin' lighter. Tell it so I can feel the warm tropical wind blowin'."

It didn't take long for me to be grateful I wasn't pulling the sled. My legs began aching, and not just from the cold. Each step was an effort. The ice was mostly solid but at times I sank down into depressions where the snow was piled deep. I could see the strain etched on the faces of the others. Just as I thought I couldn't go on another step, we stopped for lunch.

The sleds were placed close together in a line to block the wind. We ate pieces of hardtack, washed down with a thin, hot soup Cookie made. The soup traced out a path down my throat and into my stomach. It felt like the only parts of me that weren't made of solid ice.

Throughout the day I was reassured each time we passed one of the little red flags. It didn't just mean we were on the right route but somehow it seemed safer to know somebody had come before us, that we weren't the first people on this vast sea of ice.

I touched my lips softly with the end of my tongue. They stung terribly. The skin on the bottom lip was almost completely gone. Mother had put on a salve to protect it but it still hurt tremendously.

For the most part we moved along clean ice, following the marked trail. A couple of times we were stopped by pressure ridges and the men had to widen the path with pick-axes so that the bigger sleds could pass through. I was thankful for the rest while the men worked.

It was just after two o'clock when I spotted the advance party coming back to help us with our load. Some of our supplies were transferred to their two empty komatiks. We'd now be able to move much faster. It was important to get to the shelters before the last warmth of the sunlight drained away.

On reaching the shelters I felt such a sense of relief I thought I was going to cry. I needed to get inside and away from the relentless wind. I crawled into one of the shelters, slumped down on the ice and closed my eyes.

I didn't even wait until they unloaded my things.

Soon I heard voices and sat up. Jonnie was pulling in my bag and sleeping sack. I got up to help him.

"I was just coming out to get them."

"T'ought I'd save ya the work. 'Sides, just 'cause we's up 'ere don't mean a man can't be no gentleman."

"Thank you, very much. Thank you."

"You straighten out this stuff while's I go an' get the rest," Jonnie said, and disappeared down the tunnel.

Soon every part of my body, except my face, was hidden inside my sleeping sack. I was atop a makeshift bed of two caribou skins placed over my skis. This got me up off the ice, if only an inch. It was a lot more comfortable than I expected, but after a march like today's, anything would seem comfortable.

I laughed out loud as Figaro shifted around and his tail tickled my face. He was happy to be free of his little case. He settled back down into a ball and his body felt warm against my chest. Warm and reassuring. The Captain insisted he sleep with me. He said he was "darn tired of that stinkin' feline hoggin' my bed," but I knew better.

I could hear the rhythmic breathing of people sleeping in the dark all around me. There were eight of us in the shelter and our body heat warmed up the room. It was still below freezing, but much better than outside.

My lungs hadn't bothered me at all today. I hoped tomorrow I could do my share; at least take some turns pulling the sled. It wasn't fair for me to just walk while others pulled the food I'd be eating and the fuel that would warm me. But that was tomorrow. Tonight I needed to get to sleep.

I had just fallen asleep when I was awakened by a sound. At first I couldn't tell if it was the wind. Then it became louder and clearer. Somebody was sobbing. They were trying to control it, probably muffling the noise in their sleeping sack, but the sound was still escaping. I knew it wasn't Michael or Mother. It was one of the men.

The sobbing continued, but I knew nobody would try to comfort the poor soul. Tomorrow he'd rise and do the things he had to do to survive, and we'd all pretend it hadn't happened.

Helping to haul the sled might have been fair, but I found out just how difficult it really was. As the day wore on, it seemed to get harder and harder. I could feel the strain in my legs and my back and they were aching. It was a different ache from the one caused by the cold, which was always there, a dull numbing deep in the bones and muscles and joints. More than once I had to fight the desire to sit down on the ice. Each step was so heavy, I just wanted to quit, but I knew I couldn't. I had to keep moving. In only a few hours we'd reach the next set of shelters.

Once again we were following the path plotted by the advance parties. Little red markers fluttered in the ice at regular intervals. So far today I'd counted eighteen, which meant we'd travelled more than nine miles. The two crews, with the dogs and komatiks, had left before us in the morning and had beaten down a narrow path through the new pressure ridges in the ice.

It seemed much more rough today, although it might have just felt that way because I was pulling. There were pressure ridges every few hundred yards. Many of them were only two or three feet high but a few towered over our heads. And, of course, the biggest ridges all seemed to lie directly in our line of travel. The sleds came to a stop at the base of a large ridge. The men broke out the pick-axes and started to widen the path, which was big enough for the komatiks but too narrow for our sleds.

I watched them chip away and welcomed the rest, although I knew we didn't have time for this. Whether we were sitting or sledding, the sun moved relentlessly across the sky. It was more that halfway through its journey, but we weren't halfway to the shelters.

I was also worried that the two crews hadn't come back yet. By this time yesterday they'd returned and were helping us to pull the load. I stood up as the men put the pick-axes back on the sleds.

Wordlessly people fell into place. I picked up a line, right beside Michael, and, on command, we all started pulling. Slowly the sled moved up the long incline.

After some time, Jonnie yelled out, "Look!" and pointed up ahead.

We all stopped pulling. I could see two teams of dogs. They had just come around a high mound of snow and were almost on top of us.

Watching them, I was again struck by the irrational thought it was Stefansson coming back to save us. Almost as good, though. It was our advance teams returning, and we needed the help. I was afraid we'd have to make our way over the last part of the ice in darkness.

"Thank goodness," I said, to nobody in particular.

"Don't know nothin' for sure, but I don't t'ink there's much goodness ta be 'ad 'ere," replied Jonnie.

"What do you mean? They're coming back to help us."

"Ya's half right. They's comin' back but I don't t'ink

they's goin' ta be 'elpin' much."

"I don't understand," I replied in confusion.

"Look at the komatiks. Still loaded. They 'aven't dropped their supplies."

I looked at the approaching parties. He was right. The fully loaded komatiks came to a stop and the dogs collapsed onto the ice. They were breathing heavily, their tongues hanging out. It was obvious they'd been driven hard. I walked over to the Captain. Samuel Clements, the advance party leader, stopped directly in front of the Captain.

"Sir, we was hopin' ta get ta ya afore this. We didn't want ya all ta have ta travel so far an' then have ta turn around."

"Turn around? Make sense, Mr. Clements," snapped the Captain.

"No choice, Cap'n. An ice ridge has come up. Big one, right 'cross our way."

"Big? How big is she?"

"Over a hundred feet tall. We split up, tried ta find a way 'round it. It don't stop...it just don't stop."

"How far ahead?"

"A little more than a mile."

"Take the lead. I'll be followin'," ordered Captain Bartlett.

"But Cap'n, we can't be wastin' no more time...we gotta head back ta the last shelters."

"Head back? What do ya mean head back?"

"We've gotta go back ta the last shelters, afore it gets dark."

"We can't go back," Captain Bartlett said quietly.

"But we 'ave ta go back, Cap'n...we have ta be findin' shelter...we 'ave ta turn back!" Clements started yelling. His voice was frantic.

"There's nothin' for us ta go back ta, Mr. Clements."

"The shelters!" he screamed. "We 'ave ta go back ta the shelters!"

Bartlett grabbed him roughly by the shoulders. "Stop, Mr. Clements!"

"But Cap'n, ya don't understand...we gotta go back ...we gotta go back..." His voice trailed off, and he collapsed onto the Captain's shoulder. I could hear him whimper softly.

The Captain spoke quietly, so quietly I could hardly make out his voice. "Mr. Clements...Samuel...there isn't anythin' for us ta go back ta...behind us is nothin' but ice...an' death... We move forward...or we die ...do ya understand?"

"Yes, Cap'n...I'm sorry, Cap'n...it's just that..."

"No need, son, no need...it's okay...it's fine," the Captain said softly.

Mr. Clements regained his composure and the komatiks were turned around. We hauled hard to try to keep up with them. After about fifteen minutes I looked up and caught sight of the pressure ridge. From a distance it didn't look that big. Then I saw the two sleds at its foot. They were dwarfed. A mountain of ice loomed up between us and our goal.

23

We'd spent the night huddled together in three small ice shelters. It was amazing how quickly they'd been built. Under the directions of Kataktovick and the other Inuit everybody had worked together, even Michael and I. At first we'd started to build them right at the foot of the ice cliff, but the Captain ordered them to be rebuilt a hundred yards back. He didn't want the ice to crash down on top of us while we slept. As it was, we didn't have a very good night's sleep. All night long the ice "talked" loudly. The gigantic ice plates that had come together to form the pressure ridge were still pressing hard, and probably pushing the ridge higher as we slept.

Everyone was gathered at the foot of the ridge as I joined them.

"Mr. Clements, ya went 'long the ridge in both directions, is that correct?" the Captain asked.

"Yes, sir. My party went nor'-east an' Mr. Breddy took 'is ta the sou'-west. Travelled at least ten miles in both directions."

"Did either of ya see any changes in the ridge? Spots where she's lower or any difference in the ice?"

"Not a t'ing," Clements answered, and Breddy agreed.

Captain Bartlett slowly nodded his head. It was just

like the Captain to think through his words very carefully before he opened his mouth. I'd learned that the longer he took before he spoke, the more important the words would be. I swallowed hard.

"I think we have ta move an' we have ta move in a few different directions all at once. I want both of the komatiks unloaded, 'cept fer two days' supplies. As well, I want one of the sleds near empty. Put all the supplies inta one of the shelters."

"What good will it do to stay here?" asked Mr. Hadley.

"No good. We aren't goin' ta be stayin' but movin' in four ways. Two men are takin' a team 'long the ridge in one direction, while two more are ta go in the other. Four others are takin' the sled back ta Shipwreck Camp an' load up more supplies."

"That's only three directions. What's the fourth?" Mr. Hadley asked.

"Only one direction left," the Captain said. "Up an' over. We have ta start tryin' ta make a way through the ridge."

"Through? That's not possible, Robert," said Mr. Hadley.

"It has ta be possible. I don't think we're goin' ta find any other way. I expect the two teams ta come back without findin' any way 'round the ridge. We'll get over the ridge 'cause it's the only way we have." He paused. "Mr. Hadley, I want ya ta decide which of the men go which ways, an' get the parties ready ta leave while I'm climbin' up the ridge."

Mr. Hadley quickly made his decisions and the men started away with him.

"Sir, I figure ya should be takin' somebody up there with ya," Jonnie interjected.

"Ya figured right," the Captain answered. "I could use some help."

"Yes, sir, I'll get my pick-axe," said Jonnie enthusiastically as he started to move away.

"Thank ya, Jonnie, but I think we have ta figure out the best people for this job…who should go up with me."

Jonnie stopped and spun on his heels. The men who hadn't been taken by Mr. Hadley for the dog runs all gathered around.

"I'll take just one man with me…don't want ta risk more 'an one other life. Ice could fold in and bury us."

"No disrespect, Cap'n, sir, but maybe ya shouldn't be one of 'em," stated Jonnie.

"Ya got a point ta make, Jonathan?"

"Well, Cap'n, if somethin' was ta happen ta ya it'll mean desperate t'ings fer the rest of us, sir."

"The way's been set. Mr. Anderson or Mr. Hadley would take charge."

"But Cap'n, I was just—"

"Enough, Jonathan, enough! A leader has ta lead, 'specially when it's most dangerous."

"Michael! You get down from there immediately!" yelled Mother.

Every head turned. Michael was a third of the way up the mountain of ice. He hesitated for a second and then came sliding down at breakneck speed. Mother rushed over and grabbed him. She was trying to hug and swat him at the same time.

The Captain looked at Michael, and I knew what he was thinking. He walked away from the group of men towards Mother and Michael. He didn't waste any time or mince his words.

"I needs Michael ta come ta the top with me."

"Count me in!" Michael chimed in.

"Count him out!" interrupted Mother.

"But Mother!" Michael turned to the Captain. "Can't you make her let me climb?"

"Sorry, Michael. Mothers outrank Cap'ns...but, Mrs. Kiruk, I could sure enough use his help."

Mother looked from the Captain to Michael and then back to the Captain. "You said it is very dangerous?"

"Yes'm. Ice climbin' is always risky...less if the climber is light an' agile...like Michael."

"How dangerous?"

"More 'an anything we've done so far, but I'll be watching him. We'll be roped tagether. We have ta find a way through."

"Couldn't you wait until the two teams come back... maybe one of them will find a way around the ridge?" Mother asked.

"No time ta wait. If they find something then we go, but if they don't we've lost two days. We can't afford any more time ta be lost." The Captain paused and walked the few steps between him and Mother. He spoke quietly. "Michael's life...all our lives depend on gettin' over that ridge...Michael, he's the best one ta do the job. Whether he climbs or stands there isn't any safe place till we have land under our feet."

Mother loosened her grip on Michael's arm. As he started to move forward she reached out, grabbed him again and spun him around, wrapping her arms around him in a hug. Then, just as quickly as she'd hugged him, she released him.

"I have mending to do," she said quietly, and then turned and walked away. She stopped in front of one of the crude shelters, dropped to her knees and disappeared inside. I knew she simply couldn't bear to watch what was to happen.

"Jonnie, go an' get us those pick-axes an' a length of strong rope," the Captain ordered.

"Aye, aye, sir."

Michael was staring straight ahead at the pressure ridge, studying it. I knew he was trying to determine the best place to the top. I also knew he wasn't harbouring any fear or uncertainty. Michael just knew he could do it, and despite my fears, I knew he could too.

"Don't do any good ta worry, Helen," said the Captain.

"I know…but what else do I have to do?"

"Watch us climb," he said.

"I don't like to watch Michael when he climbs. It makes me all nervous."

"Nervous or not, I need ya ta do a job. Keep an eye on us. If the ice collapses, if it comes down on top of us, people have ta know where ta dig."

"Where to dig?"

"Yep. Dependin' on how tight the ice is packed, we can live for maybe five or ten minutes buried under the ice. They have ta know where ta dig. If they can't get us out fast it's just a waste a time. There's no point in diggin' us up just ta bury us again."

I felt my heart rise up into my throat. Before I could swallow hard enough to talk, Jonnie returned with the equipment. Captain Bartlett had to call Michael back. He had already started climbing the ridge again. Jonnie held up one of the ice-picks and a coil of rope. Michael slid back down the slope.

"This is going to be fun!" he exclaimed as he stopped before us.

Jonnie handed him one of the picks and then threaded the rope around his waist, tying it tightly. The

Captain tied the other end around his waist. He looked up at me.

"Keep watching us, Helen."

Roped together, they moved off to the ridge.

I watched them as though their lives depended on it, because I knew that maybe they did. Quickly the length of rope was played out as Michael scaled and scampered up the ice and the Captain was left behind. Michael moved back and forth, at times going sideways across the face of the ice, finding the best route to the top. He never slipped, or even slowed down until he got so far ahead the rope between him and the Captain grew taut and held him back like a kite that had run out the whole spool of string. He was almost halfway to the top. That seemed like the very worst place to be, neither safe at the bottom nor safe at the top.

I remembered when I was young and my parents had taken me to a travelling carnival. They thought it would be great fun for us to ride on a Ferris wheel. We climbed into that swinging basket, me in the middle sandwiched between them. I couldn't have been any more than four, but I remember it clearly. Up until the time I faced the polar bear, I don't ever remember being that scared—swinging in that little seat, suspended in the air, twirling around helplessly. Even when they began to let people off, the wheel kept starting and stopping repeatedly. I didn't think we'd ever get down. I remember burying my face into Father and suddenly feeling so safe and protected. I wished he was here now to protect me.

My eyes stayed focused on the climbers. The Captain laboured far below Michael. He swung his axe to gouge out hand- or footholds in the ice. I gasped as I saw him slip, more than once, and then regain his hold.

Slowly he crept forward until he got close enough for Michael to start climbing again. Finally, Michael disappeared over the top and I had a rush of fear. Almost immediately, though, he reappeared, and waved at me from the very top. I waved back. Within a few minutes the Captain was standing right beside him. They both waved as they moved over the edge and out of sight.

24

Carefully I held the candle underneath the bottle of ink. My hand was shaking, strained from all the hard work, and I couldn't hold it steady. The flame brushed against my fingers, but they were so numb from the cold there was no pain. I rolled the bottle and could feel it becoming liquid again. I put the candle aside.

March 5, 1914

Dear Diary,

> *I'm sorry for my shaky handwriting but it's hard to hold the pen. My fingers and my arms are aching terribly from all the digging and my knuckles are scraped and raw from where the ice has cut and rubbed and worn away my skin. We dug for five straight days, clearing a trail for the sleds over the pressure ridge. I guess I really should say the pressure ridges, because there wasn't just one, but dozens and dozens. They're stacked together just like a mountain range. Some of them were pushed together into flat plateaus, while between others there were valleys and gaps. Luckily, some gaps ran right through a couple of the ridges so we didn't have to climb them.*

> *The first day was the worst. More than half*

*the men were still out on the sleds and we were
cutting the trail up the side of the ridge. I
wanted to stop. I think everybody wanted to
quit, but the Captain wouldn't let us. Time and
again he'd offer encouragement or raise hopes.
Once he yelled at the men. They'd stopped
working, convinced we couldn't break through,
and decided we should wait until the scouting
parties returned. The Captain was angrier than
I'd ever seen him. He rained down a storm of
curse words. I've heard rough talk from the miners Father worked with but I've never heard
such language before. I was shocked, maybe
more so because it was coming from the Captain. He grabbed one man roughly by the collar
and drove him back to work. I knew he would
never treat me that way, but I dug down a little
deeper, working even harder, just to make sure I
wouldn't make him angry.*

*Digging the trail went very slowly. The men
took turns at the front, using axes and ice-picks
to chop through the ice. As the wall collapsed,
the rubble would be pushed back and used to fill
in the holes and gaps. That was one of my jobs.
All we needed was a path just wide enough for
the biggest sled to pass through. The second day
of digging was our best. We were able to clear
almost three hundred yards.*

*On the fourth day the sled returned from
Shipwreck Camp, loaded with enough supplies
to make up for those we'd used getting through
the ridges. Before they'd even unloaded, the first
of the komatiks also returned. They'd travelled
out over forty miles and there was no sign of the*

*ridge stopping. They reported, as the Captain
had thought, that there was no way around it.
Later that day the second komatik returned with
the same news. That report sent a shock wave
through everybody, but doubled our resolve to
dig. It was just as the Captain had said: dig or
die.*

*On that fifth day, with the last of the twi-
light still shining, the final section was broken
down and we found ourselves back on the ice.
The pressure ridges had been defeated, but had
it slowed us down so much the ice would melt
under our feet before we reached land? Maybe
we'd gotten through this one set of ridges but
what was to say there wasn't another, or two or
three, still up ahead?*

I don't even want to think about...

The ink had frozen solid again. I had more to write
but I was too tired to even think about it.

"Everybody take a rest!" the Captain yelled out.

I loosened the line from around my waist and
rested against the sled. Since I was in the shade I slipped
off my goggles, but the brilliant light blinded me and I
had to put them back on. There was a chill in the air
but the hard work combined with the high, hot sun
caused sweat to trickle down my sides. I loosened the
clasps on my parka to let in some air.

The sun shone down on us for more than twelve
hours a day and each day was twenty minutes longer
than the one before. By midday, the surface of the ice
was soft and we often stumbled into knee-deep slush.
There were small puddles of water everywhere.

"Here, take this."

I looked up at Jonnie, holding a canteen. I took it and tipped it to my mouth. The water tasted wonderfully sweet.

He sat down beside me. "Bad ice."

"It's always bad ice. Day after day, bad ice. There hasn't been any good ice since we hit the pressure ridge. Eight days of bad ice and yesterday was the worst."

"I 'eard we only done seven miles yesterday."

"Seven miles! We travelled a lot farther than that, I'm sure!"

"Travelled lots more 'an seven miles but only seven miles tawards the island. Today's been better ... leastways I t'ink it has. It's hard ta say how far we's movin' forward with all the ziggin' and a zaggin' round we 'ave ta do."

I knew what he meant. Not only was the ice rough but it seemed as though our path continually crossed small ridges. The Captain would set a course to avoid those that he could, but sometimes we'd have to travel more than a mile to find a way around.

Worse than the ridges, we had started to come across more and more fresh leads and open water. I was very grateful to have Daisy there to protect me. So far the leads hadn't been very long or wide but they were appearing more frequently. This was a sign the entire pack ice was starting to break up and I knew we didn't have much more time left.

"I's been t'inkin' 'bout what will 'appen at the end of this trip," Jonnie said. "Ya t'ought much about it?"

I shook my head.

"Ya gotta t'ink 'bout yer future...plan ahead like... think 'bout a husband an' such."

"A husband! I'm only thirteen," I replied.

"Only thirteen! Back where I come from some of the girls is all married an' 'avin' their first babies by the time they're fourteen or so."

"Helen, Jonnie, lend a 'and," Mr. Anderson ordered.

I was grateful for his interruption. "What is we goin' be doin'?" asked Jonnie as he climbed to his feet.

"Setting up camp," Mr. Anderson answered.

"We can't set up camp yet—it's too early," I protested. I stood up. My pants were wet from the melt water on the ice.

"No choice, Helen. Look!" Mr. Anderson said motioning into the distance. There was a column of thick, billowing clouds stretching from the ice to the sky and across the entire horizon.

"Gotta break out the skins an' put down some shelter. No time ta build with ice. Storm's comin' in...feel the wind?"

I nodded. It was blowing in strong and hard.

"Bringin' snow too. Be 'ere in less than an hour. We gotta get settled under the skins afore it gets 'ere."

"Best get movin'," Jonnie said.

The winds picked up and the sun disappeared behind the clouds. The temperature fell quickly and the snow started blowing. It was coming almost horizontally, hard and fast. It was difficult to set up the tents because the ice was so soft in places the stakes wouldn't stay in. Finally they were secured and the skins were strung up. There were only three tents and they were small.

"We can't all fit in those, can we?" I asked.

"It'll be mighty tight," Mr. Hadley replied, "but we'll fit. Helen, you and your mother should get inside and settle in. Michael, you give Kataktovick and the others some help getting the dogs settled. They'll have to be staked onto the ice."

"On the ice? In the storm? You can't leave them out! They have to have shelter!" I objected.

"The dogs'll be fine. No storm is going to bother them. Besides there isn't space for them in the tents. Don't worry, Helen, they'll be okay."

"He's right. They like the snow," Michael added.

"I've seen them fall asleep buried under a foot of snow," Mr. Hadley noted.

"But what about Daisy?"

"What about her?"

"Couldn't we just bring Daisy inside?"

"What's so special about that one?" Mr. Hadley asked.

"She's going to have puppies…soon…Kataktovick told me," I answered.

Mr. Hadley nodded. "Even if she is heavy with young she'll do fine on the ice with the other dogs. Now go."

"But what if she has her puppies tonight…in the storm?"

"She probably won't, but if she does there's nothing any of us can do about it," Mr. Hadley said, shooing me with his hands. "Nothing."

The snow was being driven under the edges and between the seams of the tent. The thin skin walls heaved and strained as the wind rattled and howled. I was afraid the whole thing would come crashing down.

Squeezed in around me, people were sleeping. I couldn't understand how anybody could fall asleep under these conditions, but I suppose everyone was just exhausted. I couldn't sleep. I kept thinking about Daisy, huddled outside in the storm. If she gave birth tonight the puppies would perish. I knew I wouldn't be able to close my eyes until I'd at least checked to see if she was all right.

Moving as quietly as I could, I started to pull myself free from my sleeping sack. I gently pushed Figaro off to the side. He'd at least keep a little part of my bed warm. Getting clear of the bedding was easy, much easier than getting out of the tent. It was almost pitch black and I was in the very centre of a lot of sleeping bodies. Carefully I stepped over and around them. The storm drowned out any sounds I made. As I unfastened the bottom buckle of the flap, I heard a voice.

"Helen, what are you doing?" It was Michael.

"Ssshhhh!" I hissed.

"Where are you going?"

"Outside... I've got to go," I answered. This was only partially a lie.

"Wait till the storm passes."

"I've been waiting, and I can't wait any longer," I whispered back.

"Daisy'll be okay, Helen, go back to bed," said Michael.

I had to smile. He knew. "I have to check. I'll be right back."

The instant the first buckle was undone the cold air blew in a trickle of snow. With the release of the second buckle the trickle became a stream. I squeezed through the opening. The snow stung against my face as I pulled up my hood and refastened the tent buckles behind me.

Turning away from the tent, I was almost blinded by the raging storm. The other two shelters, only yards away, were nearly invisible. I fought against the wind, bowing my head and pressing my body forward as I took a few tentative steps. The snow came in waves, hitting me squarely in the face and momentarily blinding me with each surge.

I reached into my pockets for my gloves. They weren't there! I'd left them in my bunk! I couldn't return for them without waking somebody up, but I knew I would get frostbite if I exposed my hands to these winds for any more than a few seconds. I stuffed my hands deep into my pockets. I wasn't going far.

I turned back towards the tents. I knew better than to lose sight of the shelters and I was relieved to make out a faint outline. The wind was now at my back and I almost tumbled over onto my face. As I shuffled backwards, looking around for the dogs, I stumbled. I tried to remove my hands from my pockets to cushion the fall, but I couldn't free them in time. I crashed hard against the ice. Then I saw what had caused me to fall—a metal stake protruding from the ice on a bizarre angle. How could there be a stake here! Stakes were driven in to support the tents or to hold the dogs in place. The dogs! This must be where the dogs had been staked out on the ice, but they were gone. The Captain's words echoed in my head: we were dead without the dogs.

I staggered to my feet. I had to get back to the tent and tell the Captain the dogs were gone. I had taken no more than two steps when I heard something. It wasn't the sound of the storm. The thought of a polar bear struck fear into my heart. I couldn't see anything in the blowing snow. I fought to keep my head up and my eyes trained ahead. Then I spotted something. At first it just looked like a series of bumps, a row of small snow drifts. Then I saw movement. It was the dogs! They were huddled together for protection from the storm.

I faced a dilemma. How could I get help without

losing sight of the dogs? It wouldn't do any good to yell; my voice would be lost in the storm. I had no choice—there was no one else but me. Maybe I could get near enough to the dogs to grab hold of the chain and drive them to the tents.

I quickly glanced back at the shelters. They were no more than twenty-five paces away. I turned again towards the dogs. At first I had trouble seeing them, but I focused my eyes and spotted them, lying on the ice, half buried beneath drifting snow. They were less than fifteen paces from me. Would I still be able to see the tents if I walked out to the dogs?

I started walking, carefully counting my steps. At the count of nine, one of the mounds of snow moved and a dog lifted its head. I froze in my tracks. I didn't want it to bolt. Slowly I brought my hands up to grab it. It wasn't until I caught sight of my hands that I remembered I was not wearing my gloves. My hands were numb, but I had to carry on.

I counted six dogs. I had no idea where the rest of the dogs were but I hoped they weren't far away. I'd get these six back to the tent and then the men could look for the others.

I no longer feared the huskies the way I had in the beginning, although I still respected their sharp teeth and unpredictability. What I did fear was that they'd run and I wouldn't be able to get them.

The six dogs were chained together and would either be captured together or run like a pack. There was no more time to think. I braced my feet and flung myself at them. The dogs yelped and jumped away in shock. I crashed with a sickening thud against the ice, cushioned by one deadened hand. Somehow my other hand clasped around the chain.

"GOT YOU!"

Before the words were even out of my mouth I realized the dogs were running and I was being dragged along.

"STOP, STOP, STOP!" I screamed.

I tried to let go of the chain but it wouldn't let go of me! The bare skin of my hand was stuck to the metal! I screamed in pain as I bumped across the ice. All at once I felt a searing pain in my side and my hand dropped off the chain. My face plummeted into the snow and I slid to a stop. My hands were red and raw and the skin had been pulled off where it had been stuck to the metal. I pushed myself up just in time to see the last of the team disappear.

I stood up and was suddenly aware that there were no dogs...no tents...nothing...except the driving snow. I had to fight the urge to run. I had to think. I knew I couldn't be more than fifty or sixty paces from the tents. Or could I? How far had the dogs dragged me? I looked for my tracks but the blowing snow had already erased my footprints. I knew the shelters were downwind so I had to move in that direction. I'd just walk straight ahead, then over a few steps and back again... but was I just moving farther from the tents and closer to freezing to death? Freezing to death! I was gripped by a cold panic that had nothing to do with the driving winds or snow.

Then I remembered that Michael had seen me leave. Wouldn't he have realized by now that I hadn't returned? He'd wake up Mother, who would wake up the Captain. They'd start a search. It wouldn't be long before they found me. Unless Michael had fallen asleep again.

I couldn't decide what to do. If I moved, I might find my way back to the tents. On the other hand, I might wander so far away they'd never be able to find me.

If I stayed put, right where I was, I would be rescued sooner or later. I might suffer some frostbite…maybe lose a toe or a finger…but they'd find me. That is, if they were even searching for me.

I couldn't make this decision alone. I needed help, somebody to talk to. Slowly I dropped to my knees.

"Our Father, who art in Heaven, hallowed be thy name…thy Kingdom come…thy will be done, on earth as it is in Heaven. Give us this day our daily bread and forgive us our trespasses as we forgive those who trespass against us. And lead us not into temptation but deliver us from evil. For thine is the Kingdom and the power and the glory, forever and ever. Amen."

As I bowed my head, I felt something press against my back and almost knock me over. I looked round.

"DAISY!" I screamed.

She nuzzled against me and then started searching through my parka, looking for a treat. I wrapped my arms around her neck and buried my face into her thick fur.

"I don't have anything for you, girl…nothing."

Daisy shifted slightly and I heard the rattle of a chain. Around her neck was a loop which trailed six feet behind her.

"Good girl, good girl."

I scratched her head behind the ears, right where she liked it. Daisy rubbed against me and I took this as a sign she wasn't going to try to run away. I dried my hand on my parka before I reached for the chain. I didn't want my skin to freeze to the metal again. I took the chain and looped it completely around my waist. Daisy wasn't going anywhere without me. I pulled her in close and huddled against her fur.

I wasn't sure how long it had been since I left the

tent. I figured I could survive out here an hour or possibly two. After that I'd be … I'd be … I couldn't even bring myself to think about it. I racked my mind for things I'd heard, stories, things I knew. I remembered stories about how you'd feel warm all over and sort of fall asleep before the cold would finally get you. I was relieved nothing about me felt warm at all. Then I recalled that awful story the Captain told us about the man freezing to death, curled up just a few feet from the shelter. I couldn't die that way.

"Come on, Daisy, come on," I ordered.

I started walking into the wind, the snow driving into my face. Each step was a struggle.

"Come on, girl," I yelled back over my shoulder.

As if the wind and snow weren't bad enough, Daisy seemed to be digging in her heels. It felt as if I was dragging her behind me.

As I moved, I counted out my steps. Ten…twenty… fifty…seventy…one hundred. And there was still no sign of anything. Nothing at all. I stopped and stared all around. Nothing. Looking back where I'd walked only seconds before, I couldn't even see any tracks on the ice.

I had to try a different direction. I started moving across the wind, the snow hitting against my left side. I'd move one hundred paces. If I didn't find anything I'd come back two hundred paces in the opposite direction.

I moved back and forth across the ice. I could see nothing. I kept walking, forcing myself to put one foot in front of the other. Daisy continued to lag and I had to pull her along behind me. What was wrong with her? Was she going to have her puppies right now?

I stopped and she came right up to me, pushing against my cheek with her muzzle. My face was so numb I could hardly feel her.

"I need you to come with me, girl…I need you to follow me," I said quietly. I was shocked at how slow and awkwardly the words rolled off my tongue.

"I'll lead us back to shelter…someplace where you can have your puppies…don't worry…you have to stop fighting me…don't fight me."

Then it dawned on me. Maybe she was fighting because I didn't know where I was going and she did.

"Can you lead us home, girl?"

She just rubbed against me. "If only I could speak Inuktituk…" I thought. Then I said, "Can you take us to the Captain…to Kataktovick?"

Daisy's ears perked up when I mentioned Kataktovick.

"Kataktovick! Go on, girl, take us to Kataktovick."

I stood up and backed off a few steps. The chain hung limply on the ground between us. Daisy didn't move.

"Kataktovick!" I shouted.

She twisted her head around, her muzzle slightly raised and her nostrils twitching. She started to move… slowly back in the direction we'd just come. I quickly followed, trying to make sure the chain didn't become taut and stop her. She picked up speed, just a gentle trot, but I found myself struggling to keep up. My whole body felt numb and heavy. The effort of picking up my feet was tremendous and I had to force myself to keep moving.

With each step, was I moving closer to the tents, or was I being led farther and farther away? So far away they wouldn't even find my body. That would be even worse than dying within sight of the tent. To be alone on the ice…not to have a Christian burial…for Mother to never really know what happened to me…I fell to the ice.

I pulled my legs in tight to my chest. I had to rest. I

couldn't go on. Besides, I seemed to be out of the wind here and it felt warmer. Warmer! I struggled to my feet once more. I had to keep fighting.

"Go on, Daisy, find Kataktovick! Go on!"

She started to move again and I dragged myself after her. I tried not to look at anything except the chain. It was my lifeline that would lead me to my tent and right into my sleeping sack, where I could close my eyes and go to sleep. Suddenly I tripped and fell. The chain was tight around my waist and I could feel myself moving. Daisy began pulling me slowly across the ice. When she stopped I looked up. There it was, only a few yards away, the tent! But I didn't have the energy to move.

The warm, soft feeling started creeping over me again. So pleasant and gentle and inviting. I thought about being in my bed at home, tucked in under my big bedspread. In the living room Mother would be sitting in her favourite chair, knitting. Father would throw another log on the fire.

"OOOUCH!" I screamed.

I was jolted out of my dream by Daisy, who was standing over me and scraping at me with one of her front paws. I pushed myself up to my knees before she could strike out again. What was wrong with that dog? Had she gone crazy? Or... was she just trying to keep me going?

I reached over and rubbed her neck. "Come on, girl, let's get inside." I managed to crawl the last few feet to the tent. I pushed my body against the opening, pressing against it with my full weight. The buckles snapped and I tumbled inside.

25

I fell onto a tangle of people sleeping inside. There was shouting and cursing at first, then someone lit a lamp.

Suddenly I was picked up like a rag doll.

"Hadley, Anderson, Kataktovick, get off her boots, an' hood and coat. Start on her limbs...we have to get the blood back in there workin'!" bellowed Captain Bartlett.

"Helen, what happened?" cried Mother. She had a look of terror on her face.

"Dogs," I muttered quietly. No one paid any attention. "Dogs! The dogs...are loose on the ice!" I called out.

Everyone stopped. "What are ya sayin', Helen?" asked Captain Bartlett.

"Stakes broke free...the dogs are loose."

"Kataktovick, take Jonnie an' get some others. Tether a long line ta the shelter an' circle out ta find the dogs. Now!"

They grabbed their things and rushed out. The cold air drove through the opening but I couldn't feel anything. I wanted to go to sleep. My eyes started to close.

"Helen, wake up!" Captain Bartlett yelled in my ear.

My eyes opened wide and I tried to sit upright but hands held me in place.

"Get the stove goin' hotter. Somebody gather some

snow and melt it down. Everybody else will be takin'
turns rubbing her limbs. We have ta work tagether or
Helen'll be...we have ta work tagether."

Or else I'd be losing my toes or fingers or worse was
what he was going to say but didn't. All around me
people were rushing. I could see them rubbing my arms
and legs and hands and feet but I couldn't feel anything.
Then, slowly I started to feel a tingle and a bit of pain.

"You're hurting me," I said feebly.

"You can feel it?" asked Mr. Hadley.

I nodded.

"Good, she's got some life! Everybody rub harder!
Rub harder!"

"Please don't! Please!" I pleaded.

"Helen, there isn't any choice. It has ta be done."

"It's time to wake up, Helen."

I opened my eyes and looked around. Except for
Mother the tent was empty.

"Get up...slowly," Mother said.

I was inside my sleeping sack on top of a stack of
skins. I pressed my hands down to try to sit up. I
screamed in pain. Part of the skin on my right hand had
been torn away.

"Is...is it going to be okay? Am I going to lose my
hand? Is it frostbite?" I gasped.

Mother pulled my head to her chest. "No dear, it's
nothing like that, nothing at all. You hurt your hand on
the chain but you don't have any frostbite."

"None? I'm not going to lose any fingers or toes?"

"Nothing. You are going to be all right. You were
fortunate you weren't out there very long, praise the
Lord."

"I'll try to get up."

Mother released her grip. I used my good hand to push off and rose to my feet. I curled my toes and moved my legs up and down. Everything seemed to be working.

"We should get outside. They want to break down the tent."

I nodded my head in agreement and started to walk to the door.

"Hold on!" Mother called out.

I turned back to face her. She held up my gloves. "You better put these on before you go outside. Remember the Captain said he'd skin you alive if you ever went outside without them again." I walked back and slipped them on.

The Captain had said a lot of things last night. Some of them not very gentle. But one thing he said stuck in my mind: because of me, they'd found the dogs.

The instant Mother and I emerged from the tent three of the men started to disassemble it. I could tell it was still early morning, because the sun wasn't far above the horizon. There was no wind. The sky above us was completely clear although there was a bank of puffy white clouds off in the distance. The air was almost warm. The blizzard was just a bad memory.

The dogs were hooked up to the sleds and komatiks. I saw Daisy and then did a quick count. All the dogs were there, hooked up in harness.

"I want everybody ta listen up!" the Captain yelled out.

Everybody stopped and turned to him.

"We're somewhere between seven and twelve miles off the coast of Wrangel Island. This is the last leg."

Smiles flashed everywhere and a couple of men yelled for joy. I felt a surge of happiness.

"But it's also the worst leg." The smiles faded. "Ice is always the most tricky near shore. More currents, open water, fresh leads an' alike. Ta make it worse the storm made a bigger mess. Ice got pushed around, snow put down over top of fresh leads. It's goin' ta be hard… real hard. We'll be keepin' tagether taday. An' in one straight line, followin' right behind each other. Less chance of somebody fallin' through the ice, that way. Let's move out."

I took my place beside the sled and we started to move. Between the bright sun and the work of pulling, I could feel sweat trickling under my clothing. I reached up and undid the top few clasps of my parka. The air felt good against my skin.

The surface of the ice was already feeling softer. This made it harder to pull the sled and I was grateful that the load was much lighter than it had been at the start of our trip.

"HELEN!"

Startled, I turned towards Mr. Hadley.

"Don't stray so far out to the side. You may be on the end of a line but I don't want to have to fish you out if you fall through…stay closer," he ordered.

I didn't need any more encouragement. I quickly closed the distance.

I saw the lead komatik come to a stop. We caught up. I was about to ask what was happening when I saw the problem. In front of us was a large gash of open water which lapped over the edge of the ice. It wasn't very wide but it extended out in both directions as far as I could see.

"What now, Robert?" Mr. Hadley asked.

"We cross it."

"And how do we do that?"

"Only two ways ta cross water. Swim or float. Anybody want ta go for a swim?" he chuckled. "Didn't think so. Guess we're goin' ta have ta use a boat."

"Boat? We don't have a boat," I said.

"Sure we do. You standin' on 'er right now." Jonnie laughed.

"I don't understand."

The Captain turned to Jonnie. "Break out the pickaxes. I'll show ya all where ta cut."

The Captain explained how this was an old sealer trick. Cut free a block of ice and it becomes a boat. The men used the axes to cut off the section of the ice on which our sleds rested. The Captain said the important thing was to make it big enough so it wouldn't tip over or flip, but not so big that it would be hard to move across the open water.

Within fifteen minutes the final pieces connecting our "boat" to the main mass of ice were cut. Using the pick-axes as poles the men pushed against the shore. At first nothing seemed to happen and then a thin dark line appeared and grew.

I felt a gentle sway. "We're floating!"

"We've been floatin' for the last six months. You just couldn't feel it after we left the *Karluk*," Captain Bartlett noted. "But we were all floatin' nevertheless."

"But this is different."

"That it is. Feels almost like being aboard ship again. Makes me a real Cap'n again," he said. There was a smile in his eyes.

Our progress over the next few hours was continually stopped by open water. The Captain guided us around two gaps, but we had to be "ferried" across the rest. It took time to chop free each ice boat. I noticed how they were cutting a smaller chunk of ice for us to stand on each time.

What I also noticed was the thickness of the ice. At the time the *Karluk* was crushed the ice was twice as thick as my height. Now it was no more than two or three feet thick. I wondered if that was just because we were cutting near an opening or if this was the thickness of the ice everywhere now. I didn't want to ask because I wasn't sure if I was ready for the answer.

The sun had made its way more than halfway across the sky already. The only clouds were the ones in the distance, now dark and stormy looking, extending right down from the sky to the ice. There was something about the clouds. They seemed to be shaded or patterned at the bottom. They almost looked like low-lying hills. I knew better than to even let my heart get excited. It was probably nothing more than a trick of the light. Captain Bartlett had told us about how Peary had thought he'd seen an entire island, ringed with mountains, which turned out to be nothing but an illusion of light and ice and clouds. Nevertheless, I kept my eyes focused on the horizon, watching those clouds. It didn't make sense, but I thought as long as I kept staring at them they wouldn't go away.

"You see it too, don't you, Helen?" Mother asked quietly. "Do you think it's real?"

"I don't know," I answered without turning my head or taking my eyes off the distant shading. "It's hard to tell."

"I've been looking at it for the past hour. The clouds shift and move but right along the horizon it stays the same. Hills…I'm sure its hills."

"You're right," interjected Mr. Hadley. "It's Wrangel Island, no two ways about it."

"Not clouds or light?" I asked.

He shook his head and smiled. "It's Wrangel...we're going to make it...thank God, we're almost there."

We stopped for supper. There was still almost five hours of daylight left. Enough light and enough time to get us onto land. It was funny how we all sat in a long row, staring at the island staring back at us. It dominated the horizon from one side to the other.

I could clearly see the low-lying hills and the mountains stretching skyward behind them. Some of those mountains were so high their tops were blurred in the clouds. We were told that in places the island rose so sharply out of the sea it would be impossible to go ashore.

Captain Bartlett, accompanied by Kataktovick, had gone ahead to mark our next steps. I'd heard two of the sailors talking about how they might find open water between the shore and the ice, and about how we could be close but not be able to land.

"Here they come," Michael announced. "And they're really moving!"

The komatik was being pulled by a full team of dogs. I could see they were coming at us at an alarming pace.

"Everybody get up and get ready to move. They're not travelling that hard to have us not ready when they get here," Mr. Hadley ordered. Instantly everyone was standing and ready to go.

The komatik slid into our midst. Captain Bartlett stopped and then bent over. His breath was coming in steamy gasps and his chest heaved up and down. People started peppering him with questions. He raised his hand and everybody fell quiet. He took a deep breath and straightened up.

"We've found a way. Ice looks like it goes clear up ta the shore. We have ta move quick. No tellin' how long before it all shifts again an' we find nothin' but open water."

Within a few minutes we were moving, led by the Captain. I was troubled by the direction we were taking. Rather than aiming straight for land we were angling sharply off to the side. The island was almost parallel to our direction of travel so we'd have to cover much more ice before we could finally touch the land. At least travelling over the ice was better than falling through it.

I kept on glancing sideways at the island. At first it didn't seem to be getting any closer. At one point I even imagined it was fading into the distance. Then almost at once it seemed we were right beside the island. We were travelling along the ice, running parallel to a high, grey, rocky cliff marking the shore. In between was a wide stretch of dark, open water and I could hear the waves crashing against the rocks. I was sure it was much too rough to even consider rafting over on an ice boat, but I didn't see any other way across it. We continued to hear the sound of the ice cracking underneath us. I wished we could move farther back, away from the water's edge. Looking forward I thought the cliff didn't seem so high.

We rounded a bluff. Stretching out before us was a blanket of white extending as far as I could see. I couldn't tell where the ice ended and the shore began, but it was clear there was no open water in between.

The men started yelling. It was apparent to everybody there was a bridge of ice stretching out before us, leading to land. Up ahead I could see the Captain had brought his komatik to a stop. Why had he stopped now?

Our sled came to rest right beside the Captain.

"Why are we stopping?" asked Mr. Hadley.

"'Cause we're here," Captain Bartlett replied.

"Here? You mean..."

"Welcome ta Wrangel Island."

26

I could feel the heat against my face. I'd never seen a bonfire this big. It was more than ten feet across and the fingers of fire reached up into the sky at least twice as high. Little embers floated up into the heavens. The snow and ice had melted away all around the fire, exposing a circle of gravel. Twice, as the fire continued to grow larger, I moved farther away, rolling back the rock which was my chair. Jonnie sat beside me as I stared at the flames—reds and yellows and oranges and blues. The vivid dancing colours were so beautiful after seeing nothing but whites and greys for so many months.

Most of the men had taken off their parkas. Two had even stripped off their tops and were undressed from the waist up. Looking at them and the fire you would have thought you were somewhere else, down south, far away from the ice. Perhaps it wasn't just me who was dreaming.

"STAND BACK!" a voice came booming out of the darkness. "MORE WOOD COMIN' T'ROUGH!"

Three men came into the blazing light of the fire carrying bundles of driftwood. As they tossed their loads into the flames, sparks and ashes billowed into the sky. When the Captain strolled into the light, the men rose to their feet, slapped him on the back, and pumped his hand.

The Captain came towards us. "Jonathan, can ya excuse me an' Helen for a couple of minutes?"

"A course, sir," Jonnie said and rose to his feet.

I squeezed over to give the Captain more space on the rock beside me. What did he want to say to me? He sat down and stared straight ahead into the fire, not talking. I felt myself getting more and more anxious. I needed to break the silence.

"I've never seen a fire this big before."

"Nice fire. Men needed the fire ta warm their bodies…an' their souls."

"It feels so nice to have the heat against my face."

"I didn't think there was this much driftwood on the whole beach. Before the night is over there won't be a stick of wood anywhere near here."

"But won't we need some wood for later?" I asked.

"Nope. There's plenty of driftwood all along the coast an' we'll only be stayin' here for the night."

"And tomorrow?"

"Tomorrow we start ta move. North an' south."

"North and south?"

"North of here about forty miles or so is where the whalin' station is located. It's on Roger's Harbour. That's where the main party is headin'."

"Main party? What main party?"

"Both sleds, one komatik, sixteen dogs, most of the supplies, all the men save two. Mr. Hadley will be leadin'."

"Mr. Hadley? But why won't you be in charge?" Of course I knew the answer before the words had fully escaped my mouth. The Captain was one of the two men going elsewhere.

"How long before you rejoin the main party?"

There was a long pause.

"I won't be comin' back, Helen."

"What do you mean you won't be coming back!" I shouted as I rose to my feet.

He reached up and took my hand. "Sit back down." I tried to pull free but he held me firmly in his grip. "Please," he said quietly as he released me from his hold.

I thought, for just a second, about walking away, but I didn't. I stood there.

"Me an' Kataktovick are headed back onta the ice."

"What do you mean? Why would you head back onto the ice. We're on land, we're safe!"

"Helen, there's no guarantee the whalers are comin' this summer. Some years they get their fill of whales farther south and don't come to the island. I can't risk having us stay here another year…or two. I have ta leave."

"But…but where are you going to?"

"Siberia. She's about two hundred miles away."

"But that's farther than we've travelled since the ship sank!"

"The two of us can travel fast…a lot faster than the whole bunch of us together. We'll be headin' out with first light, tamorrow."

"Tomorrow! Couldn't you wait a few days?"

"Can't. We have ta make it before the ice breaks up any more. It'll take us twenty days or more ta make the mainland. Then another twenty or so days till we travel down the coast ta the Bering Strait. There we can cable over ta Alaska and arrange fer a rescue ship." He stood up and reached out a hand. "Do ya understand why I have ta do this, Helen?"

"All I understand," I sobbed, "is that you're leaving us behind too." I ran off to my tent.

27

The voices floated though the thin walls of the shelter. Above the voices came the irregular yelps, barks and snarls of the dogs. They were always disagreeable when they were being put into harness.

I was alone, lying down. Everyone else was outside. I didn't need to look to know they would be clustered around the one komatik, helping to put the dogs in harness, loading the supplies, tying down the lines, and waiting. Waiting for them to leave. I'd had enough of people leaving, enough of them never coming back. I couldn't stop them from going, but I didn't have to be there to watch.

I closed my eyes and rolled over, away from the light. If I could just go back to sleep they'd be gone before I woke up again. I tried to put my mind in a happy place, to think about something else.

"Helen?"

I turned around. Captain Bartlett was partway into the tent.

"Is it okay for me ta come in?"

I didn't answer. He came in anyway.

"I just wanted ta say goodbye before I left."

He walked across the tent and sat down on the skins beside me.

"I hope ya understand, Helen. I have no choice, I

have ta go. No more choice than ya had when ya saved Michael from the polar bear."

I sat up.

"Out on the ice that night ya was in charge of your brother...the leader. A leader does what has ta be done. Same way I have ta go now. Understand?"

I nodded my head but knew this wasn't about understanding or not understanding. I just didn't want to let him go.

"I'm goin' ta miss ya. Miss sittin' down and sharin' a cup of coffee, or a game of chess, or talkin'," he paused and smiled. "Or your stories. Always liked hearin' ya tell stories."

I could feel myself start to blush. "Will I ever see you again?"

"Of course ya will! Once we all get back I'll come on up an' see ya and your mamma an' brother. Would ya like that?"

"I'd like that. I'd like that a lot."

He stood up and then offered me a hand. He pulled me to my feet. "I haven't ever spent much time with kids. I have some nieces an' nephews, but I'm always away on the seas. No kids of my own...someday I might. If I do, I hope one can be a little girl...a little girl who grows up special...as special as Helen."

I threw my arms around him and buried my head into his chest. I felt the tears start to flow again.

"Now, now, now...no need for tears."

"I don't want to say goodbye," I sobbed.

"Then don't. No goodbyes...just see ya later...that's all."

He held me at arm's length and tilted his head to one side, studying me. "Ya've come a long way, Helen."

"I guess we all have. Hundreds of miles."

"I'm not talkin' 'bout the distance. I'm talkin' 'bout a different kind of journey. I remember a little girl who came onta my ship a few short months ago. Nose buried in a book, afraid of her own shadow."

"I'm still scared."

"Be foolish not ta be scared. Don't ya think I've been scared?"

"You?"

He nodded his head. "Still am, but that doesn't stop me. The test of a person isn't that they don't get scared, but that they don't let the fear stop them from doing what needs ta be done." He paused. "Do ya think ya could do me a favour?"

"I guess so…"

"Ya see, me and Kataktovick are goin' ta be on the ice a long time. Just the two of us."

I had no idea what he was going to ask.

"Well, ya know he's a fine fella but he doesn't talk much, not much more than a few words at a time. It's goin' ta be cold…no time ta build proper shelters either. Blowing snow, ice, wind whipping up spray off the open water."

"But how can I help?"

"Tell me one of your stories."

"You want me to tell you a story?"

"Yeah, a good one."

"I…I don't know…it just seems like I don't have any stories left…it feels like I've told every story I've ever heard."

"None?"

I shook my head. "None."

"I guess I'll get by with the ones I keep up here," he said, tapping his head with one finger. "Come, it's time."

I followed him outside. There were still embers burning in the big fire pit. Everyone was gathered around the komatik. Kataktovick was beside Michael, leaning over, talking to him. I knew Michael would miss him, probably almost as much as I'd miss the Captain. I stood slightly back from the crowd and took in the scene. Farewells, words, handshakes and hugs were exchanged.

Kataktovick roused the dogs and they rose to their feet, ready to go. I looked at the Captain and he motioned for me to come to his side.

"Helen, ya was wrong."

I looked at him, completely mystified.

"Ya got at least one more story in ya. Ya just lived an adventure ... an adventure where people did things beyond belief, where men, an' a woman, an' two children refused ta stop. Where a young girl disobeyed her Captain an' returned ta a sinkin' ship ta get her diary, an' challenged a bear ta rescue her brother, an' nearly froze ta death ta save the dogs that saved everyone's life. An' this story is just a little part of a bigger story, the story of your life, the story you're living right now. Don't ever forget ya have the power ta change the pages, to make the ending different. It'll make a fine story." He smiled and then signalled Kataktovick. Kataktovick yelled out to the dogs and the team started to move.

I turned away. I didn't want to watch them disappear. I walked back to my tent and sat down on the skins. He was gone, but he'd left me something, something to help mark the time, the months that would pass before we were finally rescued.

I reached into my backpack and pulled out my diary, the pen and the bottle of ink. Some of the pages of the diary were torn and its cover was weathered. As I leafed through the pages, I found that more than half were already filled. I stopped at the first blank sheet. I dipped my pen in the thick ink.

The carriage travelled slowly through the streets...

POSTSCRIPT

❄

Robert Bartlett and Kataktovick travelled over shifting sea ice for seventeen days before they set foot on the shores of Siberia. After taking a few days to recuperate with the Siberian Inuit, they continued on their four-hundred-mile trek through the wilderness to reach the Bering Strait. From there they sent a telegram to Alaska to report the wreck of the *Karluk* and the location of the survivors. They then secured a boat to launch a rescue. The survivors, including Helen, Michael and their mother, were found on September 7, 1914.

Stefansson and the party of men who had left the *Karluk* on September 19, 1913, reached land and continued the expedition. They explored uncharted sections of the Canadian north and discovered four islands: Brock, Borden, Meighen and Lougheed. These were the last islands added to the map of the world.

The party of Alistair Mackay, Henri Beauchat, James Murray and Sandy Morrison perished on the ice. Their bodies were never found.